"What do you hope to get out of helping me?"

Lissa asked.

"I told you. Nothing."

"Don't give me that, Henderson."

"Evan. The name's Evan. And I'm not asking for anything from you."

"Ha!" Lissa flung her head back. Eyes bruised by the public scorn she'd endured glared at him. "I might have believed that three years ago. Now I know better. Tell me the *truth*, Evan. What do you want from me?"

Evan hated that she saw him with a clearer vision than he saw himself. Digging deep inside himself, he was forced to admit that he wanted a heck of a lot more from Lissa than he'd wanted from any woman in a long, long time.

Dear Reader,

This is a very special month here at Intimate Moments. We're celebrating the publication of our 1000th novel, and what a book it is! *Angel Meets the Badman* is the latest from award-winning and bestselling Maggie Shayne, and it's part of her ongoing miniseries, THE TEXAS BRAND. It's a page-turner par excellence, so take it home, sit back and prepare to be enthralled.

Ruth Langan's back, and Intimate Moments has got her. This month this historical romance star continues to win contemporary readers' hearts with *The Wildes of Wyoming—Hazard*, the latest in her wonderful contemporary miniseries about the three Wilde brothers. Paula Detmer Riggs returns to MATERNITY ROW, the site of so many births—and so many happy endings—with *Daddy by Choice*. And look for the connected MATERNITY ROW short story, "Family by Fate," in our new Mother's Day collection, *A Bouquet of Babies*. Merline Lovelace brings readers another of the MEN OF THE BAR H in *The Harder They Fall*—and you're definitely going to fall for hero Evan Henderson. *Cinderella and the Spy* is the latest from Sally Tyler Hayes, an author with a real knack for mixing romance and suspense in just the right proportions. And finally, there's *Safe in His Arms,* a wonderful amnesia story from Christine Scott.

Enjoy them all, and we'll see you again next month, when you can once again find some of the best and most exciting romance reading around, right here in Silhouette Intimate Moments.

Yours,

Leslie J. Wainger
Executive Senior Editor

Please address questions and book requests to:
Silhouette Reader Service
U.S.: 3010 Walden Ave., P.O. Box 1325, Buffalo, NY 14269
Canadian: P.O. Box 609, Fort Erie, Ont. L2A 5X3

THE HARDER
THEY FALL

MERLINE LOVELACE

Silhouette®
INTIMATE™ MOMENTS®
Published by Silhouette Books
America's Publisher of Contemporary Romance

To Betty and Dee Lovelace, who moved me to tears
with the love shining in their eyes at their
50th wedding anniversary—where, incidentally,
I first got the idea for this book!

 SILHOUETTE BOOKS

ISBN 0-373-27069-0

THE HARDER THEY FALL

Copyright © 2000 by Merline Lovelace

Visit Silhouette at www.eHarlequin.com

Printed in U.S.A.

Books by Merline Lovelace

MERLINE LOVELACE

spent twenty-three exciting years as an air force officer, serving tours at the Pentagon and at bases all over the world before she began a new career as a novelist. When she's not tied to her keyboard, she and her own handsome hero, Al, enjoy traveling, golf and long lively dinners with friends and family.

Merline enjoys hearing from readers and can be reached at P.O. Box 892717, Oklahoma City, OK 73189, or by email through Harlequin's web site at http://www.eHarlequin.com.

Look for her next book in the sexy miniseries MEN OF THE BAR H, coming soon from Silhouette Intimate Moments.

IT'S OUR 20th ANNIVERSARY!
We'll be celebrating all year,
Continuing with these fabulous titles,
On sale in April 2000.

Romance

#1438 Carried Away
Kasey Michaels/Joan Hohl

#1439 An Eligible Stranger
Tracy Sinclair

#1440 A Royal Marriage
Cara Colter

#1441 His Wild Young Bride
Donna Clayton

#1442 At the Billionaire's Bidding
Myrna Mackenzie

#1443 The Marriage Badge
Sharon De Vita

Desire

#1285 Last Dance
Cait London

#1286 Night Music
BJ James

#1287 Seduction, Cowboy Style
Anne Marie Winston

#1288 The Barons of Texas: Jill
Fayrene Preston

#1289 Her Baby's Father
Katherine Garbera

#1290 Callan's Proposition
Barbara McCauley

Intimate Moments

#997 The Wildes of Wyoming—Hazard
Ruth Langan

#998 Daddy by Choice
Paula Detmer Riggs

#999 The Harder They Fall
Merline Lovelace

#1000 Angel Meets the Badman
Maggie Shayne

#1001 Cinderella and the Spy
Sally Tyler Hayes

#1002 Safe in His Arms
Christine Scott

Special Edition

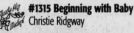

#1315 Beginning with Baby
Christie Ridgway

#1316 The Sheik's Kidnapped Bride
Susan Mallery

#1317 Make Way for Babies!
Laurie Paige

#1318 Surprise Partners
Gina Wilkins

#1319 Her Wildest Wedding Dreams
Celeste Hamilton

#1320 Soul Mates
Carol Finch

Chapter 1

If Evan Henderson had given the matter any thought at all, he wouldn't have guessed that a rangy, lop-eared jackrabbit the size of a small dog would become the instrument of his fate.

And if he hadn't spent the better part of the past week watching his brother, Jake, downing Jack Daniel's like milk, he would've kept his mind as well as his eyes on the road that curved like a lazy snake through the July heat of the Arizona desert.

But Jake's stubborn refusal to admit that he was killing himself by deliberate degrees hung like a cloud in Evan's mind. Worry about his older brother crowded everything else out and slowed his reaction time just the half second it took to turn the combination of narrow road and fast-moving jackrabbit into disaster.

The blasted thing shot out from behind one of giant saguaros that sprang up like trees in this corner of the Sonoran Desert. With a single flex of its powerful hindquarters, the oversize rodent jumped the ditch beside the road and hit the asphalt only a few yards in front of Evan's Harley XL 883 Custom Sportster. Cruising along at almost fifty, he barely had time spit out a curse before taking evasive action.

"Dammit!"

He couldn't aim left, into the opposite traffic lane. That would put the jackrabbit directly under the Sportster's wheels. His only option was right, onto the narrow, unpaved shoulder.

The instant it hit the soft shoulder, the powerful motorcycle churned up dust and bits of rock. Its front wheel fought to grab hold while the rear fishtailed all to hell and back. Evan knew he was going into the ditch even before rubber parted company with dirt. Sure enough, the Harley dived straight down and hit bottom with a bone-jarring crash. The impact sent its driver flying headfirst over the handlebars.

It wasn't the first time Evan had been thrown from a saddle. Big John Henderson had put all five of his sons on horseback before they could walk. The Henderson boys had grown to manhood riding the steep, high mountain ranges of the Bar-H. Over the years, Jake, Evan, Reece, Marsh and Sam had all collected enough broken bones and busted heads to handsomely supplement the income of their family doc in Flagstaff.

Evan had learned from those spills…and from the character-forming experience of growing up with four rowdy brothers. As handy with their fists as with a rifle or a branding iron, the Hendersons had participated in their share of barroom brawls. Instigated a few, too. Most fights they won with a show of force. Five Hendersons lined up shoulder-to-shoulder tended to intimidate even the most drunken cowboys. The few fights they'd lost generally occurred when they battled each other. As a result, Evan knew how to take a fall.

He landed on his back with a thud that rattled every bone in his body. His helmet protected his head. His jeans proved tough enough to shield his butt. The rocks and scrub brush did a number on his white cotton shirt, though. If he'd worn the sorrel-tan leather jacket he usually pulled on when cruising, he would've come out of the accident unbloodied, but the sizzling sun had made leather and heatstroke worse risks than jackrabbits.

Cursing, Evan picked himself up. His right shoulder felt like it had taken a direct hit from an iron-shod hoof, but the bones moved without grinding against each other too painfully. He rotated his arm a few times before reaching up to yank off his helmet. Spearing a hand through his hair, he surveyed the damage.

The Sportster's front wheel rim was bent almost in two, and its handlebar had twisted at an angle the design engineers had never intended. It wasn't going anywhere anytime soon.

Neither was Evan.

Climbing out of the ditch, he tugged off his sunglasses and tried to get a fix on his location. He'd come through the Gila Bend Mountains a half hour ago and passed the town of LaGrange ten or twelve miles back. Ahead...

Ahead, the road disappeared in a haze of dancing heat waves. Yuma was a good forty or so miles farther south. In between lay one or two small towns, isolated outposts baking in the July heat. And all around him, as far as he could see, were the rolling swells and purple ridges of the great Sonoran Desert.

Nothing moved in the merciless afternoon sun. No tumbleweeds drifted across the two-lane road. No hawks wheeled in the blinding blue sky. The jackrabbit who'd brought Evan down had long since disappeared. Even the rattlesnakes had sense enough to curl under the shade of the rocks during the day.

"Well, hell!"

That just about summed up the situation, he thought with a wry twist of his lips. He'd run off the road and landed in hell.

He couldn't blame anyone but himself for his predicament. He could have cruised the interstates all the way from Flagstaff back to San Diego instead of cutting across the desert. He *should* have cruised the interstates. Or left the Harley at the ranch and flown home, as an exasperated Carrie had suggested. Several times.

Carrie didn't understand why Evan had abruptly taken off with one of the biggest cases of his career about to go to the Grand Jury. Nor did she understand why he'd lingered at the Bar-H for almost a week, with nothing pressing to keep him there.

She didn't understand, because Evan hadn't told her.

He hadn't told anyone about the call he'd made to Jake last Tuesday. Or about the way his older brother had fumbled and dropped the phone twice before answering in a voice so slurred and whiskey-rough that Evan almost didn't recognize it.

He'd suspected Jake had been diving into a bottle to dull his pain long before that phone call. All of them had…he and Marsh and Reece and Sam, together with their assorted wives. Lauren, the newest Henderson bride, had picked up on it first. Maybe because she *was* the newest, because she'd met Jake at the lowest point in his life and didn't make excuses for his pain, as the rest of the family did. Or maybe her insight stemmed from the fact that the hit men who gunned down Jake's wife six months ago had gone after Lauren, too. Whatever the reason, she'd looked into his soul with the clear, keen compassion of an outsider and laid bare the truth the rest of the family had begun to suspect but hadn't yet confronted.

Evan had come face-to-face with that brutal truth this past week. He'd also learned firsthand the futility of trying to help someone who didn't want help. His last, no-holds-barred argument with Jake had been swirling around in his mind when that damned jackrabbit had jumped in front of the Harley. Now he'd pay the price for his lack of concentration.

Blowing out a long breath, Evan sidestepped back down into the ditch. The desert heat was already sucking the moisture from his body. He pulled his navy-and-orange San Diego Padres baseball cap from the saddlebag, sighing with relief when the bill cut the sun's glare to manageable proportions. Luckily he'd also picked up a couple bottles of water when he'd pulled off for gas in Buckeye and decided, like a fool, to cut across the desert to Yuma. He'd intended to use the empty stretches of back roads to think through his last confrontation with Jake.

Looked like he'd have more time to think than he'd anticipated.

He knew it was useless, but Evan tried the cell phone he always carried with him. Repeated jabs at the power button produced no dial tone. The roam function didn't work this far from a relay station. Snapping the phone shut, he stuffed it into his shirt pocket and allowed himself one small swig of the lukewarm water. Only one. There was no telling how long he might have to wait before another vehicle came tooling down the road.

Although Evan had grown up in the pine-studded high elevations around Flagstaff, he and his brothers had made enough trips south to have gained a healthy respect for the desert. There was a reason the inhabitants of the area were mostly creatures of the night. In summer, daytime air temperatures averaged around 110 degrees Fahrenheit. Ground temperatures had been known to soar to a scorching 175 degrees. Elf owls, kangaroo rats, most snakes and any damned jackrabbit with an ounce of sense hid out during the day in cactus holes, underground burrows, or any other cool, shaded spot. Which meant Evan had better find some shade, too, and fast.

The same giant saguaro that had shielded the jackrabbit drew him. Dragging his leather jacket from the saddlebag, he headed for the tree-size cactus, skirting a clump of jumping chollas on the way. The saguaro was a monster, a good twenty feet tall, with four arms that branched out about a third of the way up its trunk. Evan checked the ground around it for other shade-seeking critters before draping his jacket across two of the arms.

That done, he hunkered down in the shade to wait.

Ten, sweat-drenched minutes passed. Twenty. A half hour. He checked his chrome-faced sports watch. Carefully spaced his sips of water. Swiped the stinging salt from his eyes. He thought about Jake; about the frustrating week he'd just spent at the Bar-H; about Carrie Northcutt's impatient demands that Evan haul his butt back to San Diego, like immediately!

Resting his elbows on his knees, he laced his fingers together and pictured Carrie's delicate face surrounded by her short, feathery black hair. At first glance, she looked like a sexy, green-eyed elf. A magical creature who sprinkled fairy dust wherever she went and bewitched everyone who beheld her.

She'd certainly bewitched Evan when she'd walked into his office three months ago and announced that the Department of Justice had assigned her as special prosecutor to help him prepare the Mendoza case for the Grand Jury. Evan had never encountered such a potent combination of sensuality, intelligence and ambition.

They'd become a smoothly functioning team within a week. Become more than a team during one idiotic and incredibly erotic session on the conference table in Evan's office late one night. Carrie, being Carrie, now wanted more. Wanted—no, demanded—a commitment Evan wasn't ready to make.

He tipped his head back, squeezing another

trickle of water down his throat. With lawyerly detachment, he tried to analyze just why he kept resisting her suggestions that they pick up where they'd left off on the conference table. She didn't buy his explanation that sex and a professional working relationship didn't mix.

As she had taken to pointing out, he was the last of the Henderson brothers to bite the matrimonial bullet. Maybe his legal training had made him too cautious to enter into a binding contract he didn't have the inner drive to make work. Or maybe he was just too damned content with his free and easy life-style to alter it, as Carrie frequently claimed. She didn't pull any punches when it came to...

His hand froze with the water bottle still in midair. Was that music?

He cocked his head, straining every faculty to separate the buzz in his head caused by the heat from that distant sound.

It was music! A faint, but joyous beat drifting across the desert.

Evan lunged to his feet. Narrowing his eyes behind his aviator sunglasses, he squinted in the direction of the rhythmic beat. It took a few moments to penetrate the shimmering haze enough to spot a pickup barreling down the road from LaGrange.

Snatching his jacket from the saguaro limbs, he raced for the edge of the road. The music grew louder by the second, booming now through the stuporous heat. Evan didn't recognize the song or the artist, but that didn't surprise him. He wasn't into rhythm and blues. No, not rhythm and blues. Gospel. Rollicking, down-home, grab-at-your-gut gospel. The male vocalist climbed to impossible highs, plunged to wrenching lows and rolled every note in between in pure emotion.

"I will wait, yes, I will wait
For that pure, sweet light from above.
I'll find a way, yes, I'll find a way
To that cool, green garden of the Lord."

Evan jumped the ditch at the side of the road just as the pickup crested the same rise he'd driven over himself some thirty minutes ago. He had one arm up, slicing a wild arc through the air, when the battered white pickup sped past.

He caught a glimpse of the driver's startled face through the open side window, felt the bass beat of the music pound at his eardrums. He held his breath, waiting for the taillights to flash red as the driver braked, then cursed when they didn't.

"Hey! Stop!"

Keep going!

The thought jolted through Lissa's head even as her sneaker hovered above the brake pedal. Heart pounding, she stared into the rearview mirror at the apparition that had plunged out of the heat waves.

What she saw in the cracked mirror didn't reassure her. He was tall. Whipcord lean. Wearing tight jeans, a dirt-smeared white shirt and a navy-blue ball cap pulled low over his eyes. All that showed of his face were dark sunglasses and a tough, uncompromising chin bristling with several days' growth of beard.

Not the kind of hitchhiker any woman in her right mind should stop to pick up. Particularly a woman traveling alone down a long, empty stretch of road.

But her inconvenient conscience pinged with each turn of the pickup's wheels. The thermometer at the bank in LaGrange had registered a searing 115 degrees when she'd driven out of town. Her cutoffs and stretchy knit top were soaked with sweat, despite the wind that had rushed through the truck's open windows. The hitchhiker wouldn't last an hour out there.

Guilt piled on top of the soft heart that had gotten her into trouble more often than not. During her thirteen years at the South Oklahoma City Baptist Children's Home, the Reverend and Mrs. McNabb had taught her better than to pass by someone in need.

She speared another quick glance at the rearview mirror. Common sense and bitter experience waged a short, ferocious battle with the precepts of love, faith and simple charity.

Muttering an oath that would have shocked the good Reverend McNabb, Lissa stomped the brake.

The pedal had more play in it than the old accordion she'd first learned to pump out hymns on. She'd pressed it almost all the way to the floor before the ten-year-old pickup rolled to a stop.

She sat for a moment, both hands on the steering wheel, eyes locked on the mirror, trying to think how best to handle this situation. All the while, Marty Jones and the Silver City Quartet belted out the hymn Lissa had composed last year.

The sight of the hitchhiker loping down the road toward her galvanized her into action. Snapping off the radio, she shoved the truck into Park, but left the engine running…just in case! She shouldered open the door and climbed out. Heat flowed right through her sneaker soles the instant she hit asphalt.

"Stop right there!"

At her command, the hitchhiker slowed to a halt thirty or so yards away. What little of his face she could see under the brim of the ball cap registered approval.

"Smart lady. You're right to be cautious."

His voice rolled down the hot tarmac, deep, resonant, not dry or scratchy enough to indicate he'd been in the sun too long. He didn't sound like a bum, Lissa thought, but then her judgment when it came to scum-of-the-earth scuzz-balls was notoriously lacking.

"I'm more than cautious," she called back.

"I'm outta here if you take one more step before explaining just why you're stuck way out in the middle of nowhere."

He tugged off the ball cap to swipe his arm across his forehead. A thatch of brown hair darkened to mink by sweat glistened in the bright sun. Below it was a tanned face too rugged for handsome and too striking for any woman's peace of mind.

"I was heading south to Yuma when I got into a battle for the right-of-way with a jackrabbit. He won."

A wry grin tugged at his mouth.

Disgust tugged at Lissa's.

Even from this distance, she could see he was a charmer, just like Doc. Only younger. Sexier. Definitely sexier. Plopping his hat back on his head, he hooked his thumbs in the waistband of his jeans. His white teeth gleamed. The tanned skin beside his blue eyes crinkled with a smile that said "trust me, darlin'."

Well, she'd trusted one too-smooth snake oil salesman. She'd never trust another.

"I don't see a car," she called, her voice laced with suspicion. "Were you walking to Yuma when you lost out to that jackrabbit?"

"No, I was riding a motorcycle."

He swung a hand toward the ditch beside the road. Lissa sidestepped and caught a glint of metal.

It was a monster. One of those expensive

toys that only motorcycle fanatics or wealthy yuppies hoping to be thought really cool would invest in.

Of course, there was no saying he'd bought the thing. He could have stolen it. Or inveigled some stupid, gooey-eyed female into buying it for him.

Just like Doc.

"I appreciate your stopping," he called, breaking into her thoughts. "I know you're taking a risk. I promise, I'm not a rapist or a serial killer."

"And I'm just supposed to take your word for that?"

"My name's Henderson, Evan Henderson. I'm on my way back to San Diego after visiting family in Flagstaff. Here, I'll put my wallet down on the road. You can check my ID. My business card's in there, too."

He dug a leather billfold out of his rear pocket and dropped it onto the asphalt. Nerves jangling, Lissa watched him turn and walk back down the road.

She sucked in a swift breath at the sight of his back. A bouquet of bright red splotches decorated his left shoulder. He'd hit that ditch hard and left some pieces of himself on the rocks.

She almost called out, almost told him to grab his wallet and jump into the truck so she could get him to a hospital to clean those cuts and scrapes.

That's what Melissa Marie James, nicknamed

Lissa by the kindly Reverend and Mrs. McNabb, would have done.

Missy Marie—former child prodigy on the gospel singing circuit, crossover country music superstar and convicted felon—kept her lips clamped tight.

Chapter 2

When the hitchhiker had retreated a good distance, Lissa backed the pickup just far enough to reach his wallet. Once more she kept the truck in idle and the door open while she climbed out to scoop up the wallet. The Ford's temperamental engine spit gusts of gassy exhaust into the air, almost choking her as she studied Evan Henderson's picture on his California driver's license.

The photo didn't do him justice. The camera had failed to capture the full impact of his rugged masculinity or the smile she was sure had knocked the wind out of more than one unsuspecting female.

Swiftly she absorbed the pertinent details. Height, six-one. Weight, one eighty-two. Most of

it muscle, if his lean hips and flat belly were anything to go by. Eye color, blue. Birth date…a quick
calculation put him at thirty-one to her twenty-
seven. He was also an organ donor, which won her
grudging approval.

"My business card's in the side pocket."

She glanced up sharply to make sure he'd maintained his distance. If he'd budged as much as an
inch, she would have jumped into the pickup and
left him to broil in the afternoon sun. Although he
gave every appearance of being exactly what he
claimed—a stranded motorcyclist—Lissa had
learned the hard way not to trust her instincts when
it came to appearances.

Or men.

She dug into the side pocket to extract his card.
When the center fold gapped to reveal a wad of
bills, her stomach clenched. Doc had always carried a money roll so thick it would choke a mule.
He'd love to whip it out, particularly in front of
Lissa's fans. He'd made sure, too, the diamonds
adorning both his pinkies flashed when he peeled
off some bills.

They had to live up to her image, Doc would
say when Lissa protested the ostentation he insisted
on for both her and himself. Her fans loved show-
biz glitter and glitz. For Missy Marie, he'd ordered
thigh-skimming fringed skirts, gaudy sequined
vests that bared more cleavage than they covered,

and dramatic stage makeup. For himself, Italian suits and hand-tooled ostrich-skin boots.

Since the handsome, charismatic Doc had plucked Lissa out of the Baptist Children's Home at the ripe old age of sixteen and propelled her from the relative obscurity of the gospel circuit into a country-and-western superstar, she could hardly argue with his management plan. Although she'd cringed inside at the sequins and truly missed the uplifting nature of gospel, Lissa had trusted him with her career and her finances. The sad fact was, she'd followed his lead like a sheep to the slaughter.

Even worse, she'd tumbled into love with the handsome rat. Or thought she had. Only after he skipped town, leaving her to shoulder the blame for the illegal moneymaking schemes he ran in her name, did she appreciate her close escape. She'd also learned the bitter truth of the cliché...money really was the root of all evil. If anything, the wad Henderson carried around in his billfold made her twice as leery.

Her eyes icy, she tossed him a question. "Do you always carry this much cash with you?"

"I do when I'm traveling."

"How do I know you didn't knock off a convenience store or rob some couple parked by the roadside in their RV?"

"The money's mine."

The answer came easy, but Lissa could see that

her wary suspicion was getting to him as much as the heat. His smile lost some of its charm.

"I earned it," he said as her searching fingers found his business card. "I'm an assistant U.S. district…"

"Attorney," she read, her voice vibrating with three years of accumulated loathing.

He blinked, clearly taken aback by her venom but recovered quickly. Like all of his kind, Lissa thought on a sneer.

"I take it lawyers don't figure among your favorite people," he drawled.

They hadn't figured at all, until her arrest and trial. Just the memory of those awful days closed Lissa's throat. She'd taken full responsibility for Doc's scams. How could she do anything else? He'd used her name to bilk a legion of trusting fans out of sums ranging from as little as five dollars to as much as several thousand. It had taken everything Lissa had left after Doc disappeared with the money he'd stolen, but she'd repaid most of the angry victims. As a result, she'd received probation instead of a jail sentence.

She didn't blame anyone but herself for her stupidity in trusting Doc. Acknowledging her own culpability didn't, however, make it any easier to stomach the lawyers who'd roasted her on a judicial spit. They ranked right up there with the media who'd subjected her to such a savage public pillorying.

She had to fight the urge to leave this particular snake out here with his scaly desert brethren. It was a fierce battle. Spinning on one heel, she grabbed the open door of the truck to haul herself up.

"Get in," she called coldly over her shoulder.

"Thanks."

Blowing out a long, relieved breath, Evan closed the distance to the pickup. The tang of hot tar bubbling between the cracks in the road stung his nostrils. The flashing scorn in his rescuer's eyes when she'd read his card stung his pride.

Like all members of the bar, he endured his share of lawyer jokes over the years. A few, he appreciated for their wit. Most, he shrugged off. He gained too much satisfaction from putting the scum he prosecuted behind bars to worry about jokes.

So why the heck did it bother him what this long-legged, tumble-haired blonde thought of his profession? Obviously she'd knocked up against the legal system at some time in her life. You didn't grow that kind of aversion by watching from the sidelines.

He climbed into the pickup, grimacing when the heat from the sun-baked plastic seat burned through his jeans, and slammed the door.

"We've established my identity," he began as he caught the wallet she tossed him. "Care to tell me..."

She gunned the engine. The pickup shot forward. Evan's head jerked back, hitting the rear window with a thump.

"...yours?" he finished, his mouth tightening.

She didn't answer. White-knuckled, her hands gripped the wheel. Her eyes drilled the empty landscape ahead.

Evan had to admit they were incredible eyes. Cinnamon-brown with thick lashes, under delicate, arching brows several shades darker than her sun-streaked tawny hair. She'd pulled the shoulder-length mane back in a loose ponytail, but enough strands had escaped to frame high cheekbones and a short, straight nose lightly dusted with freckles.

But it was her mouth that grabbed Evan's attention and wouldn't let go. He guessed her lips were full and luscious when they weren't pressed into such a tight line. No lipstick, he noted. No makeup at all, in fact. Not that she needed it with that soft, creamy skin tinted to a golden brown by the sun.

She looked vaguely familiar, although he was sure he'd never met her before. He would have remembered her striking face. Not to mention the body that went with it.

He let his glance drop, following the line of her throat to the full, high breasts covered in stretchy blue knit. His eyes lingered on the slice of bare skin between her top and the waistband of her cut-offs. Funny, he'd never thought of the midriff as a particularly erotic portion of the female anatomy, but his rescuer's dips and hollows and tiny, curled belly button stirred a definite spark of masculine appreciation.

And her legs. God, the legs stretching out below those ragged cutoffs contained more long, smooth curves than Evan had seen in…

"Lissa."

He yanked his gaze back to her stony profile. "Okay, I'm listening."

"Not listen. Lissa." Swiping back her wind-whipped bangs, she fired him an impatient look. "My name is Lissa."

"Oh. Right."

She didn't offer a last name and Evan knew better than to ask for one. The woman might possess the body of a sun-kissed goddess, but that sexy collection of curves came packaged with the personality of a cactus.

"The ditch runs out a little way up ahead," she said curtly. "I'll turn around and take you back to the hospital at LaGrange."

He wasn't about to impose on her more than he already had. "I don't need a hospital. Only a phone to call my road service."

"Those scrapes on your back should be looked at."

"They're okay. What's up ahead?"

"Paradise."

He hooked a brow. Despite his reputation as a prosecutor who'd slice right to the jugular of a lying witness, he couldn't tell whether or not her response was a sarcastic reference to the locale.

She caught his questioning look and offered a grudging explanation. "Paradise is what's left of a mining town. It's about three miles further south."

"I didn't see anyplace by that name on the map."

"You wouldn't. It disappeared from most maps a decade or so ago."

Which was exactly why Lissa had chosen it as her sanctuary. Tiny, dusty, deserted Paradise, set smack in the middle of the hottest stretch of nowhere God had put on the earth. Its isolation provided her the obscurity she craved, the total anonymity she'd needed to lick her wounds.

"Does Paradise have a phone?" her passenger asked. "And somewhere I can get a cold drink?"

"There's a café of sorts in the gas station. It has a pay phone."

"Then I don't need to take you out of your way. You can drop me off in Paradise."

He smiled when he said it, his lips curving in a way that invited her to share in the joke. Lissa kept her eyes on the road and her mouth set.

She hoped he'd take the hint. She should have known a lawyer couldn't resist poking and probing.

"Are you from around here?" he asked a moment later.

"I am now."

She coated the words with ice to discourage further conversation, but the truth of her reply warmed her inside. She'd found peace in the dry, dusty isolation of Paradise. A measure of contentment she hadn't thought she'd ever achieve again. For three years now, she'd whittled away at her remaining debts by composing and selling songs under a pseudonym. For three years, she'd recovered from the shame of her trial in total obscurity.

Except…

Lately Paradise hasn't seemed as peaceful or as isolated as when she'd first arrived. A couple of times she'd glimpsed a car parked at the edge of town. Just last week, the mongrel who'd taken up residence under her trailer had set up a furious racket. Recently she'd had the eeriest feeling she was being watched when she picked up the mail and royalty checks Mrs. McNabb forwarded to her in LaGrange. She might have dismissed the feeling as pure nerves if she hadn't been sure her mail had been tampered with.

The idea that someone might have tracked her down, might be lying in wait for her, made her stomach curl. She'd buried herself in Paradise to escape the hordes of reporters and angry fans she'd let down…not to mention the small army of talk show hosts and con artists who'd descended on her like locusts after the trial. They refused to believe the millions Doc had scammed in her name had disappeared with him. At the time, a stunned Missy Marie couldn't believe it, either.

Older and far wiser now, Lissa couldn't imagine how she'd ever been so naive.

Suspicion settled hard and cold in her chest. Was this Evan Henderson really who he said he was? Had he been sent by one of the talk show hosts or magazine editors who kept pestering her through the mail forwarded by Mrs. McNabb, trying to entice her back into the public eye? Had he planted himself out here in the middle of the desert as a ruse, intending to intercept her when she'd come cruising back from La Grange?

She aimed a quick glance at her passenger. He was an attorney, if she could believe his business card. An assistant D.A. He swam in the same waters as the legal sharks who'd ripped her apart three years ago, but there was no reason to believe he'd come in search of her. She'd paid her debt to society. Most of it, anyway. A few more hit songs and she could breathe free again.

Evan caught her speculative look and returned it with one of his own. Propping his arm on the open window frame, he stretched out his legs as far as the stick shift and rusted floorboards would allow.

"You look familiar, but I know we've never met before. I would have remembered."

So would she. As much as her experience with Doc had turned her off men in general and smooth-talking charmers in particular, she would have remembered Evan Henderson. After all, she wasn't dead. Only gut-shot and gun-shy.

"Maybe we bumped into each other on the street somewhere," he mused when she didn't answer. "Have you ever been to San Diego?"

Lissa gritted her teeth. The last thing she wanted was to engage in small talk with this too-handsome stranger. As she knew from bitter experience, however, a stony silence provided no protection against a lawyer's relentless, sometimes savage inquisitions. Besides, she'd only fire his curiosity if she kept silent.

"No."

"Flagstaff?"

"No."

He cocked his head. "Not particularly inclined to conversation, Ms....Lissa?"

"No."

His blue eyes laughed at her even as they raised little flicks of nerves under her skin.

"Okay. I'll just sit back and enjoy the view."

She whipped her head around, ready to lay into him. Giving the man a ride didn't mean she had to put up with the kind of sexual innuendoes she'd endured when Doc had decked his sixteen-year-old protégée out in spandex and spangles and touted her as a sultry voiced Lolita.

To her chagrin, she saw that Henderson had been referring to the view outside the truck window, not the one she provided in her skimpy cut-offs and tank top. He'd turned his head away, presenting her with his chiseled profile. The wind whipped his hair, more tobacco than mink in color now that the sweat had dried. Crinkly little lines formed at the corners of his sunglasses as he narrowed his eyes against the glare.

Despite herself, despite every agonizing lesson she'd learned three years ago, Lissa couldn't entirely repress a little twinge of feminine admiration. Evan Henderson was a hunk, plain and simple.

Her mouth tight, she swung her gaze back to the road ahead and pressed down on the accelerator. The sooner she got him to Paradise, the sooner she could dump him.

The abandoned bauxite mine came into view first. The gray, weathered buildings where aluminium had been stripped from ore dug out of the earth now clustered forlornly amid a lake of heat waves. Tumbleweeds had piled up against the fence surrounding the facility. Desert sand coated every horizontal surface.

The town that had almost died when the bauxite ore played out lay a mile farther south. Constructed of the same weathered gray wood as the processing plant, its handful of buildings strung out along a wide, dry arroyo. Lissa had lived in Paradise long enough to appreciate the blinding speed that arroyo could fill with water. Storms broke maybe two or three times a year in this corner of the desert. But when they did, the sunbaked earth couldn't absorb the downpour. According to the locals, the only death that had ever occurred in Paradise was a coyote caught by the rushing water in the arroyo.

Lissa wheeled the pickup down the town's single street, imagining how her sanctuary must look to someone seeing it for the first time. Boarded-up windows stared like blind eyes from what used to be the town hall/post office. A sign with its lettering scoured completely off by wind-driven sand hung by one hinge above a former coffee shop.

Henderson's low whistle cut through the heat. "You weren't kidding. This place is a ghost town."

"Almost. A few people stayed after the bauxite plant shut down."

A very few. Three or four old-timers, who'd lived through the boom and bust of the fifties. A one-time Las Vegas cigarette girl who'd left the glittery city after her husband of one week dropped dead while dealing a hand of seven-card stud. Charlie Haines, who owned the only commercial establishment still operating in town, a sort of garage, general store, restaurant and bar all rolled into one.

The small community had taken Lissa in without too many questions. A few brows had lifted when she'd moved into the dilapidated trailer on the edge of town, sure, but she'd dodged the questions until they petered out and had come to feel safe. Safe and blessedly anonymous. Lissa didn't want any outsiders violating her sanctuary.

Particularly this outsider.

She didn't like his rugged good looks, didn't like what he did for a living, and surely to goodness didn't like the way he stirred something deep in her belly she didn't want stirred.

Lissa hadn't been this edgy around a man since… She set her mouth, forced herself to finish the thought. Since Doc. And for reasons totally unfathomable to her at this point, Evan Henderson bothered her almost as much as her memories of her sleazebag manager.

With every breath she drew in Henderson's scent, a combination of heat, wind and healthy male. His jean-clad knees practically knocked hers in the close confines of the truck. She couldn't wait to get him out of the pickup and out of Paradise.

Antsy with the need to be rid of him, she drove past the few inhabited houses at the north end of town and pulled up at the native stone building known as Charlie's Place.

"There's a phone inside," she told Henderson. "And a bar of sorts where you can get something cool to drink."

Nodding, he reached for the door handle. Lissa bit her lip at the sight of his torn shirt and bloodied shoulder. She'd offered once to take him to La-Grange to get those cuts and scrapes tended to. She wouldn't offer again. She'd done her Good Samaritan duty for the day.

He swung back, smiling at her through the open door. "Thanks for the ride."

She dipped her head in curt acknowledgment. That was the best she could do with his blue eyes lazy on her face and his shirt gaping open at the neck to reveal gold-tipped chest hair glistening in the sun.

"I'd like to pay you for your trouble."

"I don't want your money."

"It's come by honestly," he reminded her with a grin as he reached once more for his wallet. "Please, let me pay to get your truck's air-conditioning fixed. It's the least I can do by way of thanks for saving my skin."

Jaws tight, Lissa shoved the pickup into gear. "I don't want your money."

The pickup's worn tires spun. She peeled away, leaving Henderson in a cloud of thick, choking dust.

Chapter 3

Muttering under his breath about a certain dewy-skinned blonde with the poisonous temperament of a Gila monster, Evan swept off his ball cap and beat the dust from his sleeves and chest.

"Watch what you say 'bout Lissa, boy."

The deep, scratchy voice came at him through the screen door of Charlie's Place. The speaker was an indistinct blur, lost in the contrast between the blinding glare outside and the building's dim interior.

"What did you do to rile her?"

"Nothing," Evan said shortly, pounding at his thighs with the cap. "Except try to thank her for giving me a lift."

"She's a mite touchy around strangers," the disembodied voice rasped.

"So I noticed."

"When you get right down to it, most of us here in Paradise are."

"Well, this stranger's moving on as soon as he gets hold of his road service." Cool, damp air seeped through the screen door, drawing Evan like the song of a siren. "Mind if I use your phone?"

"Not if you buy a beer or two while you're using it."

The screen creaked open. Gratefully Evan pushed through. He stood for a moment just inside the door while his pores gulped in moisture-laden air. From the water rivulets making tracks on the fly-specked mirror behind the bar, he guessed the owner had installed a water-fed swamp cooler, the kind that worked better with windows and doors left open a crack to circulate the damp air.

When his senses had made the transition from searing brightness to dank dimness, he turned to the short, stocky individual in grease-stained overalls. "Are you Charlie?"

"That's me."

The old man's crankshaft voice had to be the product of too many cigarettes and too much desert dust. Beetle-black eyes almost hidden by folds of weathered skin looked the newcomer up and down.

"Who are you, boy?"

Evan beat back a smile. The only other person

who still called him "boy" was Shaddrach Mc-
Coy, the leather-tough foreman of the Bar-H
who'd refereed too many of the rambunctious Hendersons' free-for-alls to count.

"Evan Henderson," he replied, thrusting out a
hand. "I'm from San Diego, by way of Flagstaff."

Charlie gave him another once-over, then took
his hand in a callused paw. Evan managed not to
wince at the crushing grip and instantly revised his
estimate of the proprietor's age downward by a
decade.

"What do you do in San Diego?"

"I'm an assistant U.S. district attorney."

"That so?"

Charlie's glance shifted to the screen door. Outside, the plume of dust made by the white pickup
still swirled on the hot air. When he turned back
to Evan, his lined face was unreadable. If he shared
the same low opinion of attorneys Lissa obviously
did, he didn't voice it.

"About that beer...?" Evan prompted. His
throat felt as dry as an old saddle blanket and twice
as scratchy.

Ambling behind the makeshift bar wedged into
one corner, Charlie hauled out a longneck and
thumped it down on chipped gray Formica.

Evan's parched throat convulsed in anticipation.
Aside from the water he sipped in the shade of the
saguaro, he hadn't put any liquid inside him since
his last cup of coffee with Jake early this morning.

Lifting the bottle in a silent salute, he chugged a good third of the icy beer.

Arms spread, beefy palms planted on the Formica, Charlie waited until the bottle lowered to resume his interrogation. "How'd you hook up with Lissa?"

"I lost out in a game of road chicken with a jackrabbit and left my Harley nose down in a ditch. Lissa stopped to pick me up."

"Blamed-fool thing for a female ridin' these roads alone to do, if you ask me. But that's Melissa James for you. The girl's always pickin' up strays."

Melissa James. The name suited her, Evan thought. It reminded him of the whisper of the wind through the cottonwood trees. Or the hiss of a diamondback just before it struck. More curious than ever about the contradictory woman who'd stop for a stranded hitchhiker, yet never crack a smile the whole time she hauled him into town, he initiated a casual probe.

"What other strays has she picked up?"

"The flea-bitten mongrel who's taken up residence under her trailer, for one. Old widow Jenks, for another." Shaking his shaggy gray head, Charlie swiped the wet ring on the Formica with his forearm. "That soft heart of hers is gonna get her in trouble all over again."

Again?

So Evan's initial guess had been right. His

prickly rescuer's aversion to lawyers obviously stemmed from something more than general prejudice.

"Lissa mentioned that she lives here in Paradise now," he said idly, implying a far more extensive conversation with her than the curt monosyllables she'd grudgingly let drop.

"If you call camping out in that old trailer livin'. Danged thing should have been hauled off to the scrap heap years ago."

Interesting. She lived in an old trailer. Drove a pickup that sported more rust than paint. Yet she'd turned down flat Evan's offer of payment.

Intrigued despite himself, he hooked a heel on the rungs of a chrome bar stool topped with a tattered red plastic seat. With the consummate skill of a prosecutor considered the front runner for U.S. district attorney when his boss retired next year, he set about to extract more information from Charlie. It didn't take him long to discover that the few remaining residents of Paradise, Arizona, had taken Lissa James under their collective wings.

"You must have said something to rile her," Charlie commented with a shrewd look. "Never seen her drive off and leave someone in the dust like that. Most times, she's as sweet-tempered as an angel."

Evan refrained from comment.

"Take the way she feeds that half-wild mongrel. Or the way she fills in as organist when they need one at the church over to LaGrange. She's all giving, that girl. There's not a mean bone in her body."

Her luscious, long-limbed, very seductive body.

Evan tipped back his beer, remembering all too well the play of muscle and smooth, tanned skin when her legs had shifted away from his. Remembering, too, the pale splash of freckles almost lost in her tan and that pouty, all-too-kissable mouth.

She'd certainly made a hell of an impression on him, he admitted with a silent grin. Not that his interest sprang solely from lust. More from a awareness of Lissa James as an intriguing, desirable woman on one level, and a mystery to be solved on another. Or so he tried to convince himself when he accepted Charlie's offer to reclaim the Harley.

"We don't get many travelers down this way," the barkeep/mechanic commented, "but there's no sense leaving a prime piece of machinery like that lying abandoned alongside the road. I've got a winch on my wrecker that'll lift her out of that ditch. Between the two of us, we can muscle her into my truck and haul her back to Paradise until your road service gets here."

"Sounds like a plan to me."

"There's a rack of T-shirts in the corner over there. You might want to pull one on before you go back out in the sun."

"Good enough. I'll get changed, make a couple of phone calls and be ready to roll."

While Charlie went out to throw some equipment into his tow truck, Evan downed the rest of his beer and considered the limited selection of souvenir T-Shirts. Grinning, he opted for a neon yellow with Wile E. Coyote racing across his chest in full pursuit of the Road Runner. It wasn't as macho as the bloodred model sporting a salivating, mean-eyed rattler, but it would do.

Tossing his torn shirt into the trash, he made two quick calls. The first was to his road service, which promised to pick up the motorcycle in Paradise and transport it to the nearest Harley repair facility. They'd also send a car for Evan.

The second was to his office. His assistant, a sharp young paralegal attending law school at night, answered on the fourth or fifth ring. Sharon sounded even more frazzled than usual.

"Jeez, boss, it's absolutely crazy around here."

"When is it ever anything else?"

The harried assistant relayed a request for his immediate return from his boss and an annoyed demand from Carrie Northcutt to know where the hell he was. Apparently she'd been trying to reach him for the past several hours on his cell phone.

"I'm taking the scenic route home," Evan replied with a laconic glance around the dim, dank bar. "My cell phone doesn't work out here in the desert."

"Desert? Where are you?"

"About an hour north of Yuma, at a forgotten spot on the map called Paradise. What's got the boss in a buzz?"

"The mayor's putting pressure on him. He wants an update on the Mendoza case."

Since the mayor himself had hired one of the illegal aliens imported by Hector Mendoza's well-oiled, well-financed smuggling organization, Evan wasn't surprised that the anxious politician wanted to be kept informed on the status of the case. The mayor claimed complete ignorance of his house-keeper's illegal immigration status, as did the dozens of other wealthy employers scattered from Beverly Hills to La Jolla. They also all swore they knew nothing of the drugs these unsuspecting mules carried into the States with them.

"Ask Carrie to start putting an updated brief together. I'll go over it with her when I get back."

"Which will be…?"

Evan aimed a frown at the mirror on the wall behind the bar. He still felt edgy, still hadn't worked through the worry over Jake that had taken him off the interstate and onto the back roads to think. Adding to that worry was a curiosity about his rescuer that seemed to have grabbed hold of him.

"I'll be back as soon as I can."

"But…"

"Today's only Friday. I'd planned to be out of the area until Monday, remember?"

"I wished you'd remind Carrie of that," Sharon muttered. "She's been on my case all day."

Beautiful, brilliant, brittle Carrie Northcutt wasn't a favorite among many of the women in the D.A.'s office. Or among a good number of the men, either. As she'd told Evan with a careless shrug, she didn't have time to pander to personalities.

"Tell Carrie I'll call her later," Evan instructed. "And run a background check on a woman named Melissa James for me, will you? She's twenty-five, give or take a couple of years, around five-six, one hundred and twenty pounds, blond hair, brown eyes."

Technically Evan shouldn't ask his assistant to run a background check without cause. But his instincts told him there was more to Lissa James than her sun-streaked tawny hair and touchy disposition, and Evan had learned long ago to trust his gut.

Promising to call Sharon back later, he tugged on his ball cap and braced himself for the sledge-hammer blow of the heat outside.

The sun was blazing low on the horizon when Lissa strolled into town that evening.

She often walked this time of day. She ran in the mornings, while it was still cool, but got out to watch the spectacular desert sunsets paint the sky whenever she could. Before she'd come to Paradise, she'd never seen such symphonies of colors, all golds and purples and swirling, triumphant reds. The wonder of them had found its way into more than one of the hymns she'd sold under her pseudonym the past few years.

The shower she'd taken a half hour ago had lifted the layers of sweat and road dust from her skin. A floppy-brimmed straw hat shielded her face from the last of the sun's rays. She'd exchanged her cutoffs for an ankle-length gauzy skirt dotted with pink flowers that matched her sleeveless pink vest.

She always wore a skirt to visit Mrs. Jenks. The frizzy-haired, onetime Las Vegas cigarette girl certainly wouldn't object if Lissa appeared at her door in skimpy cutoffs. But all those years at the Baptist Children's Home had left their mark. A body didn't go calling on neighbors in shorts.

Not that Lissa would label her twice-weekly visits to Josephine Jenks calls, exactly. Mostly she went to deliver the mail she'd picked up for the elderly widow in LaGrange...and to dust her porcelain cats. Josephine had collected almost three hundred of them over the years, and her eyesight wasn't as keen as it used to be. After she'd knocked two of her favorites off the shelf, Lissa had volunteered to take over dusting duty. She didn't mind the hour or so it took to clean the porcelain figurines. It was little enough price to pay for Josephine's fussy, funny companionship and a slice of her killer spice cake.

Humming a fast, uplifting hymn in six-eighths time, Lissa decided to detour into Charlie's Place. She'd meant to drop off his mail earlier, but in her hurry to dump Henderson she'd forgotten it.

"Hey, Charlie."

Chilled air flowed over her like cool satin as she pushed through the screen. Reaching into her skirt pocket, she pulled out the advertisements she'd retrieved from Charlie's post office box in LaGrange.

"I've got your…"

She stopped dead in her tracks. Her stomach knotting, Lissa glared at the figure sitting with one boot hooked on the lower rung of a chrome bar stool, his spoon raised over a half-empty bowl of Charlie's infamous armadillo and green chili stew.

"What are you doing here?"

Henderson swung his head, a dark brow lifting at her sharp tone. "At the moment, I'm trying my best to convince myself this is really chicken I'm spooning down."

The smooth reply came with a lazy smile that had no doubt enticed more than one eager female down the path to perdition. Lissa had already traveled that road. She wasn't about to make the trip again.

"I thought you were heading back to San Diego."

"I am. Eventually."

Evan pushed around with his heel, wondering why the devil this woman irritated and intrigued him in such equal measures. He could have told her that he and Charlie had manhandled the Harley out of the ditch and into his truck. That they'd gotten lucky and found a replacement wheel rim in a junkyard in LaGrange. That he'd called his road service and canceled his request for a car, intending to hit the road again as soon as Charlie finished changing the old rim for the new.

Instead he leaned an elbow on the chipped Formica and tried to recover from the gut-clenching impact of Melissa James all combed out and cleaned up. Evan couldn't quite figure out how, but her long, swirly skirt and demure little vest carried even more of a kick than the thigh-skimming cutoffs and bare midriff she'd worn earlier.

Dusty and windblown, she could have modeled for a bust of a bronzed desert goddess. Now, she looked like every man's dream of the girl next door grown to sensual, stunning womanhood. Her dark gold hair fell in a sleek curve to her shoulders. Under her veil of bangs, wide brown eyes flashed a message of unmistakable wariness.

Once again, the feeling that he knew her tugged at Evan's mind, like the refrain of an old, half-remembered song. He wished to heck he'd called Sharon back for the results of the background check before settling down to a bowl of this dubious stew. He'd do that later, after he voiced the apology he'd been chewing on for most of the five hours since she'd driven off in a whirl of dust.

"I'm sorry I offended you this afternoon."

"Not everyone expects payment for a simple act of kindness."

"I know. I'm sorry," he said again.

She unbent a little. Not enough to smile, but at least the suspicion faded from her face. "Apology accepted."

Without the sharp edge, her voice rippled with low, musical notes. Like a trickling mountain stream, Evan thought. Or a satin ribbon fluttering in the breeze.

"At the risk of putting my foot in it again, can I buy you a beer or a soft drink? Or—" he cast a doubtful glance at his bowl "—some dinner?"

That did the trick. Her lips tugged upward. A glint of laughter danced in her eyes. The physical change was so slight, yet the overall result so profound, that Evan forgot to breathe.

"You're braver than I am," she confessed. "I've never had the nerve to try Charlie's stew."

"It's not bad…if you don't let yourself think about it too much while you're eating."

A perverse and wholly unexpected urge gripped Lissa. To her surprise, she found she wanted to take him up on his offer. Wanted to slide onto the stool next to his, plop her elbows on the counter and let down her guard an inch or two. It had been so long since she'd relaxed. So long since she

shared a conversation with a man her age who
didn't regard her as either a superstar selling sex
with her songs or a criminal.

With some effort, she repressed the traitorous
urge. She knew she had to turn around and walk
out. Right now, before she said or did something
to destroy the fragile cocoon she'd spun for herself
these past few years.

"Thanks, but I'll pass on both dinner and a soft
drink. I just stopped in to drop off Charlie's mail."

Depositing the advertisements on the counter,
she turned to leave.

A ridiculous sense of disappointment spiked
through Evan. She'd almost unbent. Almost
laughed. For some absurd reason, he wanted to see
her do both. Never one to give up without a fight,
he tried one more time.

"Look, I know I came across as a jerk when I
offered to pay you this afternoon. I think you
should give me a chance to recover. I'm not always
that gauche."

"You didn't strike me as gauche," she admitted.
"Maybe a touch…"

"Cynical?" he supplied when she hesitated. "I
guess maybe I am. I've spent too many years prosecuting the bloodsuckers and leeches who prey on
others. Dealing with scum like that tends to give
you a jaundiced view of human nature."

Before his eyes, she stiffened up again. Too late,
Evan remembered his earlier suspicion that she

must have come down on the wrong side of the
law at sometime in her past. He cursed his slip
when her teeth came down hard on her lower lip.
Cursed again when an emotion very close to pain
flashed across her face.

He searched for some way to blunt the effect of
his careless comment, but before he found it, she
whirled and headed for the door.

"Lissa, wait!"

She palmed the screen with a thump and sailed
outside.

Calling himself ten kinds of a jerk, Evan started
after her. He yanked open the screen and strode
into the blinding light, only to collide full force
with a stiff, rigid Lissa. She'd stopped again, was
standing rooted to the spot like a pillar of salt until
Evan crashed into her.

Some fancy dancing and a quick arm around her
waist kept them both from going down. As soon
as he'd found his feet, she twisted furiously in his
arms.

"Sorry," he began for the third time in as many
minutes. "I didn't mean to..."

"You snake!"

"What?"

Her eyes spit fury. The color that had drained
from her cheeks only moments ago rushed back
with a vengeance.

"You low-life sidewinder! You couldn't wait to
sic the hounds on me, could you?"

She wrenched out of his hold, or tried to. Belatedly Evan realized he was hanging on to her with the same wary grip he'd once used to pick up a hissing, spitting bobcat kitten.

"What hounds? What are you talking about?"

She jerked away, her face flushed with fury. "I supposed I asked for it when I picked you up." Scorn and self-disgust darkened her eyes to almost black. "One of these days I'll learn."

Her bitterness lashed Evan like a whip. It didn't help that she'd directed it as much at herself as at him.

"Learn what? What are you talking about?"

"That!"

Flinging out her hand, she indicated the van parked at the rusted gas pump. Decorating its side panels was the colorful, instantly recognizable NBC peacock.

"I'm going out the back way," Lissa spit out furiously. "If either you or the driver of that van try to follow me, I'll...I'll make you wish you hadn't!"

Chapter 4

A furious Lissa retreated into Charlie's Place, leaving Evan staring blankly at the van. While he debated whether to follow her or check out the vehicle, a fragmented conversation reached him.

"...seen her?"

"No."

That was Charlie. Gruff and rusty as a leaking pipe. Evan started forward.

"But..."

"No, I said."

"I had a report she might be somewhere in this area," the unseen speaker pressed. "I just want to ask her a few questions."

Evan rounded the front of the van, his eyes nar-

rowing on the pencil-thin, hunch-shouldered reporter in tan Dockers and a blue knit shirt sporting
the call letters of a California TV station.

"Ask who a few questions?"

The newcomer spun around. "Missy Marie," he
said eagerly. "The country singer who scammed
all those people a few years ago. Have you seen
her?"

With the mental equivalent of a thunderclap, the
pieces tumbled into place. Melissa James...
Melissa Marie. The tousle-haired sex kitten who
fell from the galaxy of country singing stars with
a crash.

A burst of TV images from her sensational trial
flashed through Evan's mind. The accused's
strained, heavily made-up face. Her hollow state-
ment that she didn't know anything about the deals
worked in her name. The angry recording mag-
nates, the music video producers, the disillusioned
fans, all demanding their money back.

Evan recalled, too, the shots of her slick, absent
manager. Evidently the jury believed he'd engi-
neered most of the illegal scams, since they'd let
the star herself off with a suspended sentence.

Evan hadn't paid a great deal of attention to the
details of the case, other than to skim the sum-
maries in the monthly Department of Justice report. The trial had been handled by federal prose-
cutors out of the Nashville district. His own

workload kept him busy enough without getting sidetracked by cases outside his jurisdiction.

"I got word she might be around here somewhere," the reporter repeated. "Have you seen her?"

Beyond the thin, eager man's shoulder, Evan caught Charlie's stare. He didn't need the warning in the mechanic's black eyes. Lissa had paid her debt to society. She'd also stopped to rescue a stranded biker this afternoon. He owed her.

"Missy Marie?" he replied with a shrug. "No, I haven't seen her."

It was the truth, if not exactly truthful. Even now, knowing who she was, Evan had a hard time connecting the kittenish singing sensation sporting mountains of teased hair, spiky fake eyelashes and overdone stage makeup to the woman with the scrubbed, freckle-splashed face who'd picked him up this afternoon.

"Why are you looking for her?" he asked slowly.

"I did a piece on her when the case first broke. I want to do a follow-up. I'm Dave Hawthorne, by the way. I work for WKML in L.A."

He fished around in his shirt pocket for a business card. Evan skimmed it, then handed it to Charlie.

"I got a tip a few months ago from a Nashville affiliate that Missy had settled somewhere in southern Arizona or California," the reporter continued.

"I've been trying to track her down ever since. As I said, I want to do a follow-up. You know, a sort of before and after to see if the gospel singer-gone-bad has found forgiveness and redemption. Although…"

He shoved his tiny round sunglasses up his sweat-slick nose and glanced around.

"I guess she wouldn't be hanging around here if she had. Particularly not if she made off with any of the millions she and her manager raked in from all those suckers."

Evan dragged his memory for the details of the sensational case. "I thought the defense established that she hadn't received any of the money."

"Yeah, well, maybe she did and maybe she didn't. You know how juries are. A pretty woman turns on the tears, they believe anything."

Evan could speak to the vagaries of juries with a heck of a lot more authority than Hawthorne, but he wasn't about to get into a debate over the judicial system.

"Just out of curiosity, what made you think Missy Marie was here in Paradise?"

"I can't reveal my sources."

The pompous reply nicked Evan's temper. Judging by the way Charlie's lip curled, it nicked his, too.

Hawthorne realized he wasn't winning any points with either of them. Abandoning the high ground, he plastered a conspiratorial smile on his face.

"Actually I've got a buddy who works for the IRS. He put a flag on Missy Marie's computer file. Her address is blocked in the system per a court order, but anytime there's an inquiry about her, my friend calls me with a heads-up."

"Convenient," Evan commented.

"Yeah, isn't it? An inquiry came in this afternoon, giving her last known location as Paradise, Arizona. I didn't have anything else to do, so I thought I'd drive out to poke around."

Well, hell! The routine background check Evan asked Sharon to run would've included a financial status query. Lissa was right, after all. All unknowing, Evan had sicced the dogs on her...just as she'd accused him of doing! Guilt nipped at him, and he decided he'd better throw this particular dog off the scent.

"In case you're not aware of it," he drawled, "accessing IRS data systems without proper authorization is a misdemeanor punishable by a fine of up to $5,000 and possible jail sentence of six to nine months."

Hawthorne's smile slid right off his face. His glance dropped to the roadrunner racing across a field of neon yellow on Evan's chest, then back up to lock with cool, unfriendly eyes.

"Are you a cop?"

"I'm an assistant U.S. district attorney with the 3rd Circuit, Southern California district."

The reporter paled, but quickly recovered. "The Southern California district? That's San Diego, isn't it?"

"It is."

"So what are you doing out here in the middle of nowhere?" Like a ferret digging furiously into the burrow of his prey, the reporter's narrow face sharpened. "Is the D.A.'s office hunting for Missy Marie, too?"

"No."

Only one particular person in the D.A.'s office, and right now he was kicking himself royally for allowing his curiosity to pry the lid off Pandora's box.

"Then why are you in Paradise?" Hawthorne demanded.

"I'm just passing through," Evan replied with deceptive casualness. "On my way back to San Diego. When I get there, I might just ask my staff to check into this buddy of yours at the IRS."

"Hey, c'mon. I told you that off the record."

Charlie weighed in then, his voice as gritty as desert sand. "Well, this here's *on* the record. There's no one 'round here like this Missy Marie person you describe. A girl passed through yesterday, some sassy blonde drivin' a flashy Jag XJS, but she only stayed long enough to gas up and use the john."

"Did she say where she was headed?"

"I didn't ask. We don't go pokin' and pryin' into other folk's business here in Paradise." His black eyes bored into Hawthorne. "Unlike some people, who don't mind breakin' a few laws while they're at it."

"Look, I didn't... That is, I don't usually—"

Ruthlessly Charlie cut him off. "You'd better not start diggin' into my tax records, boy, or I might just have to drive into L.A. with my 12 gauge and take the matter up with you personally. Now do you want some gas for this van or are you just wastin' both our time?"

"I don't need any gas."

"Then git."

Hawthorne got. The van door slammed behind him. The engine gunned.

Evan stood shoulder to shoulder with Charlie until the van was nothing more than a small speck against the blazing red ball of the sun. As soon as the vehicle disappeared, their united front crumbled.

Charlie turned to Evan, his weathered face set. "I s'pose you figured out that Lissa is this Missy Marie. Or used to be."

"Yeah, I figured it out."

"Why didn't you tell Hawthorne?"

"I owed her for the favor she did me this afternoon."

"And you always pay your debts?"

"Always."

Scrunching his lids to filter out the sun's slanting rays, Charlie studied the man standing before him with legs spread and boots planted wide in the dust. The mechanic had been around some in his sixty-plus years, enough to go with his gut when it came to other folks. He'd taken Henderson's measure this afternoon during the drive out to retrieve his bike. Sensed he could trust him. The past few minutes had proven him right.

Maybe the Almighty had sent that jackrabbit skittering into Henderson's path for a purpose. Maybe this man was the answer to the worry that had grown in Charlie like a cancer these past few years. Wasn't right, a young woman like Lissa hidin' herself away in the desert. Wasn't right she had no one to look out for her 'cept him and Josephine Jenks and the few other residents of Paradise, all of them with one foot in the grave.

Charlie believed all things happened for a purpose, including a bent motorcycle wheel rim. He rocked back and forth on his heels, thinking, while Henderson reached for his wallet.

"Speaking of payment, what do I owe you for the stew, the shirt and the bike?"

"Well, now..." Dragging a rag out of his back pocket, Charlie rubbed at the grease on his palms. "I've been wrestling with that rim we got over to the junkyard in LaGrange. I'm afraid it's dented some, too. I'll have to straighten it out before I can put it on your bike."

"How long will that take?"

"Can't say for sure. Couple of hours. Maybe longer." He took a final swipe and tucked the rag back into his pocket. "You might as well plan on bedding down here in Paradise tonight."

"In Paradise?"

His brows soaring, Evan shot a glance down the deserted main street. The empty buildings and boarded-up windows didn't promise much in the way of accommodations.

"Widow Jenks has a spare room she rents out to the EPA inspector when he comes out to check the mine," Charlie informed him. "She can put you up for the night."

Evan swallowed the protest that jumped into his throat. He'd spent enough time in the mechanic's company this afternoon to reject the idea that he was trying to hold him up for more money to fix the Sportster. If Charlie said he needed more time, he needed more time.

Evan needed time, too, to apologize to Lissa. Again.

It was becoming a habit, he thought ruefully.

Widow Jenks lived in a cement block fifties' era house at the far end of main street.

Instead of the kindly, white-haired lady Evan had envisioned, his hostess greeted him at the door in rhinestone-trimmed glasses, a low-cut black leotard showing massive mounds of wrinkled bosom, and leopard-print capri pants that matched the color of her frizzy orange hair. The overall effect was awe-inspiring, but Evan soon discovered that Josephine Jenks's personality overpowered even the capri pants.

"Charlie called and said it was okay to take you in. Do you like cats?"

"It depends," he answered warily. "Will I have to sleep with one?"

"One?" Her snort of laughter didn't exactly reassure Evan. "Come on in, Henderson."

Wondering what in the hell had he gotten himself into, he followed her into a living room so crowded with knickknacks that he kept his elbows jammed tight into his sides for fear of knocking something over. They were all cats, he saw. Ceramic. Cloisonné. Plastic. Wooden. Some even carved out of what looked like dried fruits and vegetables. To his immense relief, the only live feline he spotted was a monster that spread like a white, furry inner tube across most of the sofa. The thing must weigh a good twenty pounds.

The room at the back of the house his hostess showed him to was spotlessly clean. It was also decorated with another menagerie of cat figurines. Evan only hoped the unwinking eyes staring down at him from every horizontal surface didn't keep him awake all night.

Propping a plump, leopard-covered hip against the doorjamb, Josephine watched while he dumped the saddlebags on a chair and dug out the few toiletries he'd packed for his week at the Bar-H.

"Charlie tells me you come from up around Flagstaff."

"My family has a spread about ten miles from the city."

"How big a spread?"

Evan hooked a brow, but answered easily enough. Within minutes, Josephine had extracted his birth date, rank order among his siblings, marital status, length of time in his current job and approximate income.

Seemingly satisfied, she retreated, only to cut him a razor sharp look when he came out of the bathroom some time later, showered and shaved.

"I need to stretch my legs."

"Well, there's plenty of room to stretch them around here." Her crimson-tipped fingers combed the monster's white fur. "But if your stretching should happen to take you up to Lissa's trailer…"

"Yes?"

"Just remember she's got friends here in Paradise. Good friends who don't want to see her hurt more than she already has been."

"I don't plan on hurting her."

What, exactly, he *did* plan puzzled the heck out of Evan as he strolled through the balmy night. First, he'd have to admit that he'd inadvertently alerted Hawthorne. Second, he needed to reconcile in his own mind the wounded dove Charlie and Josephine described with the nubile young sex goddess whose manager had scammed millions in her name. And maybe…just maybe…he'd also satisfy this itchy need to understand why she'd hidden out in the back corner of nowhere all these years.

The public was notoriously forgiving. Movie and recording stars got busted every day on charges ranging from paying for sex to murder, as did their counterparts in sports and politics. Most returned to the limelight almost immediately. But not Lissa James. That intrigued Evan almost as much as the memory of the smile he'd teased from her earlier this afternoon.

Following a trail of molten moonlight, he climbed the rocky path that led up to a trailer perched on a rise overlooking Paradise. Giant saguaros dotted the slope, raising their arms to the heavens like ancient Druids offering pagan prayers to the moon.

Light spilled from the trailer's windows. Light and music, Evan discovered when he was halfway up the slope. He paused, head cocked to catch the faint strains.

Unlike the pounding, rhythmic hymn that had boomed through Lissa's truck windows this afternoon, this one floated on the moonlight, soft and wrenchingly sad. Evan couldn't quite make out the lyrics…something about a splinter from the cross, he thought…but there was no mistaking the singer.

He knew nothing about music. Even less about gospel music. For the life of him, he couldn't say whether Lissa was a soprano or an alto, or even what the difference was. He recognized artistry when he heard it, though. She sang without amplifiers, without backup, without the synthesizers that mixed sounds and poured out electronically enhanced versions, but the soft, silvery notes reached into his soul.

He followed the music up the hill until, suddenly, a snarl cut through it.

Just as suddenly, a dog burst from under the trailer. A very large dog, Evan saw as the dark shadow streaked toward him. Its furious barking brought the trailer door crashing back on its hinges.

Lissa stood framed in the light. "Wolf! What's got into you now?"

Wolf? Evan didn't like the sound of that. He liked even less the sight of the shaggy creature's bared fangs. His every muscle knotting, he tensed for the attack.

"Down, Wolf!"

The animal slowed its charge as Lissa screeched another command.

"Down, boy! Down!"

To Evan's profound relief, the dog dropped to its haunches less than a yard away, quivering from its black-gummed muzzle to its bent tail. The fangs stayed bared. The ruff stood straight up. The snarls emanating from deep in its throat put up the hairs on the back of Evan's neck, as well.

"Who is it? Who's there?"

Lissa's sharp cry carried over the rattling growls. Evan wrenched his gaze from the canine to the woman silhouetted in the open door. Her golden hair spilled over her shoulders. The curves outlined through the gauzy material of her skirt spiked a pulse already hammering from the dog's lunging attack.

"It's me. Evan."

She didn't answer for long, long moments. He figured she was waging a fierce internal debate over whether or not she should let her dog go for his throat.

"What do you want?"

"I came up to apologize...again."

"Save your apologies, Henderson. They're not worth diddly."

"I didn't call that reporter and tell him you're in Paradise."

"Ha!"

"But I might have inadvertently given him a clue to your whereabouts."

"Inadvertently my big toenail!"

Despite himself, Evan had to grin. Between his brothers and the criminals he'd prosecuted over the years, every four-letter word in the book had been hurled his way at one time or another. But he couldn't remember anyone ever tossing that one at him. He took a step forward, almost forgetting the snarling animal. The creature instantly reminded him who was in charge.

"Call off your dog, will you? I'd like to…"

"I don't care what you'd like. I don't want anything from you, Henderson."

"I know. You made that clear this afternoon. But I owe you at least an explanation…and the assurance that I'll rectify my error."

"It's too late. The story's probably already made the evening news. By tomorrow, the vultures will be circling overhead."

"Maybe not. Let me come up, Lissa. We'll talk about it."

He knew just the right chords to strike, she thought with an angry twist to her mouth. Just what drops of hope to sprinkle in her direction. He knew darn well she wouldn't turn him away if there was a chance she might not have to leave her sanctuary.

Lissa had never thought of herself as a coward. She'd lost her mother to a car accident when she was three, her father to cheap booze and unbearable heartache a year later. She hadn't cried when he'd left her in the street outside the Baptist Children's Home, hugging a ragged Pooh Bear and foolishly believing with childish faith his promise that he'd come back for her soon. Nor had she sorrowed all those years at the home. The Mc-

Nabbs had lavished such love on their charges, she
refused to repay them by pining.

Besides, she'd had her music. The barely remembered lullabies her mother had hummed. The
joyous hymns the congregation sang at worship on
Wednesday nights and Sunday mornings. The battered old accordion the McNabbs had somehow
scraped together enough to buy for her seventh
birthday, recognizing they'd taken something of a
child prodigy under their wing.

Even when Doc had come along and swept her
away from all she knew, Lissa hadn't been afraid.
She'd gone with him without a second thought,
eager to share her songs of faith with the world.
Eager, too, for the paternal kisses he showered on
the all-too-gullible sixteen-year-old.

The turbulent years that followed had opened
her eyes considerably. Toughened her, as well. So
much so that she'd endured the shame of her trial
without shedding a tear.

But now...

Now she'd found peace. A peace she'd pay just
about any price to keep. Including, she admitted
on a ragged sigh, opening her door to Evan Henderson.

As she stepped outside to convince Wolf to let
him pass, she couldn't shake the feeling that Henderson constituted far more of a threat to her hard-
won tranquillity than any reporter.

Chapter 5

Wolf didn't take to strangers any more than the other residents of Paradise. After several minutes and a litany of sharp commands, he finally dropped his gums back over his fangs, ceased growling and slunk into the shadows.

Lissa's uninvited guest uncoiled his muscles and slowly approached. "Nice pet you've got there."

"He's not mine," she replied with a snap. "He's just sort of…taken up temporary residence under the trailer."

Temporary equated to just over a year now, but Lissa made no claims to ownership of the half-wild animal. In retrospect, she probably shouldn't have fed him that night he'd knocked over her garbage can. The crash had scared the dickens out of her, but when she'd kneeled on her bed to peep through the blinds, one glimpse of the raider's mangy fur and washboard ribs had wrung her heart. She'd climbed out of bed and emptied the fridge of leftovers. Cracking open the trailer door, she'd tossed them outside.

The animal had returned two nights later, skittering away when Lissa put out more food and a bowl of water, then wolfing down both with a voraciousness that eventually earned him his name. She couldn't begin to guess where he'd come from, or what his ancestry was. His short, pointed ears and long muzzle hinted at German shepherd but his mottled brown/black coat was too long and shaggy to qualify for that breed. Lean and rangy as a coyote, he looked like he'd survived months, if not years, in the desert.

Over the ensuing months, Lissa and the dog formed a loose partnership. Very loose. Wary and skittish, he allowed Lissa to feed him and talk to him occasionally. In return, he slept under the trailer and provided a strangely reassuring presence during the long, empty nights. Not that she'd needed reassurance here in Paradise.

Until lately.

Her mouth tight, she remembered the prickly sensation that she was being watched in LaGrange earlier this afternoon. Remembered, too, Wolf's furious, unexplained barking last week.

Now two strangers had arrived in Paradise on the same day. First Henderson, then the reporter. According to Charlie, the reporter had left with a flea in his ear. The next step, she decided, was to get rid of Henderson.

Nerves jangling, Lissa climbed the two front steps of the trailer. Her uninvited guest followed her inside. His broad-shouldered presence filled the tiny eating space she jokingly called a dining room. He'd showered and shaved she saw...and was immediately, intensely irritated with herself for noticing.

She closed the front door with a snap to capture what remained of the butane-cooled inside air. When she turned, her stomach lurched. Henderson's glance had fallen on the hand-scribed music score sheets scattered across the table that served as dinette, desk and stand for her electric keyboard.

His glance lifted to her, curiosity rampant in his blue eyes. "I know now you're a singer, but I didn't realize you also compose. Did you write the hymn I heard you singing before Wolf launched his attack?"

"No."

It wasn't a lie...exactly. She hadn't composed that hymn. She was still in the process of composing it. Snatching up the score sheets, Lissa slapped them face down on the table.

No one knew about the songs of faith she wrote and sold under a pseudonym. After all, what gospel singer wanted to record a piece written by someone who'd shamed herself and her music? Gospel had become a multimillion-dollar business, and vocalists chose the material they recorded with great care.

The lead titles on *Southern Gospel Singing*'s Top Eighty Chart grossed almost as much for their artists as a platinum hit grossed for many of today's top rock groups. Legendary greats like bass vocalist J. D. Sumner, listed in the *Guinness Book of World Records* for recording a double low C on two separate occasions, had started small and made music history. Vocal groups such as the Jordanaires, the Blackwood Brothers, and the Stamps Quartet, who'd toured with Elvis Presley, had helped found the Gospel Music Association and turned the genre into the booming industry it was today.

Now hundreds of radio and TV stations across the country played the unique combination of pop and religion. Thousands of vocalists poured their hearts and souls into songs of faith. Despite that, gospel singing still remained a relatively tight community. One that guarded its ranks jealously. Lissa should know.

Her crystal clear vocalizing and joyous renditions of the old hymns had rocketed her to the top of that close-knit community while she was still in her early teens. She'd left it at Doc's insistence to make the crossover into country. Now she was back, composing the music she loved under an assumed name. She didn't need a nosy lawyer poking into her business...and destroying her fragile peace.

"The song was beautiful," he said, not the least put off by her curt response. "What's it called?"

She hadn't got around to a title yet. Annoyed but now stuck with her semitruth, she grabbed one out of the air.

"'One-Way Ticket to Paradise.'"

His mouth lifted. "Appropriate."

Bird feathers and brimstone! There it was again. The lazy, crooked smile that invited her to join in the fun and laugh with him. Lissa refused to acknowledge the answering quiver deep in her belly.

"You said you wanted to apologize and explain. Why don't we skip the apologies and go straight to the explanation?"

"Fine."

Uninvited, he made himself at home in the only armchair the trailer boasted. Her lips tightening, Lissa took the dilapidated sofa. A crocheted throw covered most of its nauseous yellow plaid, but the lumpy couch still topped her list of items needing replacement as soon as she paid off the last of her debts.

"Well?" she asked frostily.

"I asked my assistant to run a check on you."

A slow hiss escaped her lips.

"I couldn't shake the feeling that I knew you,"

Evan admitted with a shrug. "You stirred my curiosity this afternoon."

She stirred a lot more than that, he confessed silently. From the first moment she'd swung those long legs out of the truck to check his ID, she'd triggered a chain reaction. In the space of a single afternoon, he'd run the gamut from interest to intrigue to an annoying, itchy attraction that just wouldn't quit.

Take right now, for instance. Evan had to fight to keep her swish of honey-colored hair and hostile brown eyes from completely derailing his thoughts. Not to mention the delectable curves buried under yards of gauzy skirt. With considerable effort, he yanked himself back to the business at hand.

"Unfortunately, the routine query my assistant ran tripped a flag."

"What kind of a flag?"

"A buddy of our friend, Hawthorne, put a special tag on your IRS file."

Dismay battled with anger on her expressive face. "But my tax records are supposed to be blocked! The court ordered the IRS to shield them when one of the men Doc scammed came after me with a—"

She broke off, biting down on her lower lip.

The unfinished sentence tied Evan in knots. Like most of the professionals dedicated to preserving law and order, he sympathized with victims denied justice by legal technicalities or slick, high-priced defense attorneys. Too often for his peace of mind, these dissatisfied victims attempted to extract a personal revenge when the system failed them. The thought of one of those angry defendants coming after Lissa with a knife or a gun put a kink in his gut.

"According to Hawthorne, your records are still blocked. But my assistant's query gave your last known location as Paradise, Arizona. That alerted Hawthorne's pal, who called him and put him on your trail."

"Thanks a lot." The sharp-edged scorn in her voice could have cut glass. "The next time I come across a stranded hitchhiker, I'll leave him to broil in the desert sun."

"Under any other circumstances," Evan said wryly, "that's exactly what I'd advise you to do."

Not that she'd follow any advice he offered. If half what he remembered from Missy Marie's sensational trial was true, she was at worst a conniving scam artist, at best a gullible twit.

But Lissa James...

According to the residents of Paradise, a vulnerable heart beat in that luscious body. If the Widow Jenks was right, Lissa could no more drive by a stranded motorist than she could run a scam.

"Between us, Charlie and I threw Hawthorne off the scent. I don't think he'll be back."

Particularly if the reporter found himself facing possible criminal charges. Evan wouldn't bat an eye at holding that threat over Hawthorne's head to keep him away from Lissa.

"Charlie told me how you threatened the guy," she acknowledged grudgingly.

Frowning, she pleated the filmy material of her skirt between two fingers. When her eyes lifted to his, suspicion and anger still lingered in their depths.

"Why didn't you tell him about me?"

"Isn't it obvious?"

"The past few years have taught me not to trust the obvious."

As a prosecuting attorney, Evan would have to agree she'd learned a valuable lesson. Yet a part of him regretted she'd had to learn it the hard way.

"I owed you, Lissa. I'm not the kind of man to repay a kindness with betrayal."

The look she gave him suggested that she knew a few who would. Her absent manager headed the list, no doubt. Evan made a mental note to request the background file on her case when he got back to San Diego. He wanted to find out more about the man who'd left her holding the bag. Find out, too, why the heck he hadn't been brought to justice along with Lissa.

"Were you watching me in LaGrange?"

The terse question jerked him out of his thoughts. "What?"

"This afternoon, in LaGrange. Did you stop for

gas on your way through town? Maybe see me there?''

His brow lifting, he took her query one step further. ''Then hotfoot it out of town and stage that accident just to get you to stop?''

Red flowed back into her cheeks. She must have heard the touch of paranoia in her question. Or the ego of a star used to being part of a brilliant galaxy. Anyone whose orbit included a small army of managers, publicists, recording executives, costume coordinators, hairdressers and a legion of adoring fans might fall into the trap of thinking she was the center of their universe.

Evan had spent enough time in this woman's company now to dismiss both paranoia and ego as the basis for her unexpected question.

''If I'd spotted you when I cruised through LaGrange,'' he answered slowly, ''I certainly would have sat up and taken notice. Maybe even tried to engineer a meeting. But I didn't.''

Frowning, she worked more pleats in her skirt with nervous fingers.

''What made you think someone was watching you?'' he probed.

She'd roused his professional as well as his personal interest now. When she didn't answer, he pulled it out of her.

''Come on, Lissa. You can't hint that I ran my bike into a ditch to stage a meeting with a beautiful woman and just drop it there.''

If the compliment registered, she didn't show any appreciation. A frown creased her forehead when she met his eyes.

"It was only a feeling, okay? A sort of itchy sensation."

Her tight, defiant tone dared him to dismiss her itch as neurotic.

"I'm listening."

She chewed on her lower lip, obviously needing to talk, just as obviously reluctant to talk to *him*.

"At first I thought someone in LaGrange had recognized me. I kept looking over my shoulder, thinking I'd spot whoever it was. I'd just convinced myself I was imagining things when you appeared in the middle of the desert. Then that reporter showed up..."

The flowery fabric wadded into a ball under her nervous fingers. Evan couldn't help himself. Stretching out a hand, he gently pried her fingers free and took them in a loose hold. The contact surprised her as much as it did him. Her startled glance jumped to his face.

"There's more, isn't there?" he guessed.

He'd nailed it. He could tell by the way her fingers trembled before she jerked them from his grasp.

"Tell me," he urged.

"Why? What possible concern is it to you?"

Evan was darned if he knew. He improvised,

trying to justify his trek up to her trailer tonight to himself as much as to her.

"I'm a good listener, and a pretty good lawyer. I'm also stuck here until Charlie fixes my bike. Maybe I can help you with whatever's making you so nervous."

"Why?" she asked again, her brown eyes hostile. "What's in it for you?"

"Nothing. I'm just trying to make amends for almost bringing the hounds down on you."

"By dispensing free legal advice? I don't think so." She sprang up, her shoulders stiff. "If you're thinking to cash in on some of the money that disappeared with Doc, you'd better think again. I don't know where he is, don't know where the blasted money is and don't care."

"Lissa…"

"I've paid back almost every penny," she interrupted fiercely. "With interest! It's taken me three years, but it's nearly done. At this point, I don't care if Doc and his stolen loot dropped into a crack in the earth and went straight to…to Hades."

He surged to his feet, not nearly as amused this time by her quaint expletives.

"Dammit, I'm not looking for a share of this so-called loot."

"No? Then maybe you think you can convince me to go back into the business. Maybe you want a piece of the new, reformed Missy Marie. You wouldn't be the first," she said with withering scorn. "I had my fill of agents and promoters urging me to cash in on all that great publicity generated by my trial."

God! Her scars ran deep. Controlling himself with an iron will, he kept his voice level.

"I'm the last person who'd urge you to exploit your trial and conviction for gain. I'm a public servant, remember? We government types don't particularly enjoy watching outsiders make millions off cases we sweat blood over."

"Then what do you hope to get out of helping me?"

"I told you. Nothing."

"Don't give me that, Henderson."

"Evan. The name's Evan. And I'm not asking for anything from you."

"Ha!" She flung her head back. Her hair swept her shoulders. Eyes bruised by the public scorn she'd endured glared at him. "I might have believed that three years ago. Now, I know better. Tell me the truth, *Evan*. What do you want from me?"

He hated that she saw him with a clearer vision than he saw himself. Digging deep inside himself, he was forced to admit that he wanted a heck of a lot more from Lissa than he'd wanted from any woman in a long, long time, Carrie Northcutt included.

"All I was hoping for was another smile," he

tossed back. "You've got one heck of a smile, lady…when you unbend enough to let it off the leash."

Her brows slashed down. Disbelief and scorn rang in her voice. "You expect me to believe that's all you want? A smile?"

"It was until a few moments ago."

"I thought so!" Folding her arms across her chest, she glowered at him. "All right. Spell it out in layman's terms, Counselor. What's the real charge for this legal advice you're offering?"

"A kiss, for starters."

"What?"

She took an involuntary step back, startled out of her scowl by his blunt reply. Her fish-eyed surprise sparked a streak of pure deviltry in Evan. She wanted the truth? He'd give it to her, without spit or saddle polish.

"A long, slow kiss. With mouths open. Teeth knocking. Tongues tangling. The kind my brother Marsh used to call a Saturday Night Special."

She backed up another step. "You're out of your mind!"

"Could be."

He followed, noting with great interest the flush that started at the V of her pink vest and surged upward. Noting, too, the stab of pulse at the base of her throat.

"A man would have to be crazy to wrap his arms around a woman as prickly as a cactus," he murmured, fascinated by that throbbing pulse. "Or ache for her to wrap hers around him."

Considerably encouraged by the fact that she didn't haul off and slug him, Evan planted a palm against the faded pecan paneling beside her head.

"But holding you is high up there on the list of what I want from you, Ms. James. Right alongside a Saturday Night Special."

The man was insane! Lissa couldn't believe he was standing there—no, *leaning* there—smiling down at her while he laid out those outrageous conditions! Any more than she could believe she was standing here with her back to the wall, shaking like a knock-kneed ninny at the mere thought of sharing a long, slow, tongue-tangling kiss with this stranger.

A moment ago, she was ready to toss him to the wolves. Or at least to Wolf. She didn't trust his offer of help. Wasn't sure she believed his too-ready explanation of the reporter's unexpected appearance. Nor could she bring herself to accept Charlie's gruff endorsement, which had surprised the heck out of her.

Yet here she was, torn by the same need for human contact that had pierced her at Charlie's this afternoon. Aching with a need that curled low in her belly. Wanting to reach up, wrap her arms around Henderson's neck and deliver one doozy of a Saturday Night Special.

The sad fact was that she'd only kissed one man

in her life. Two, if she counted the affectionate pecks on the cheek she'd given Reverend McNabb. Maybe three. She'd probably planted some childish kisses on her father before he'd deposited her on the road outside the Baptist Children's Home.

But Doc... Doc had played her like a twenty-dollar fiddle. Looking back, Lissa cringed inside whenever she remembered how eagerly she'd accepted his careless kisses. How she'd forced herself to ignore the teachings of a lifetime and respond to his hands on her young, untutored body. How hard she'd tried so hard to convince herself she was in love with him.

Yet never, ever, had she felt this wild, sweet need to touch, to taste, to simply lose herself in the thrill of wanting and being wanted.

"I think..." She forced the words through a throat gone tight and dry. "I think you'd better leave."

Okay, Evan told himself sternly. He could do this. He could drop his arm. Pull away from her. Walk out of the trailer.

It was harder than he could ever have imagined. His jaw ground so hard it ached. Sweat filmed the back of his neck. Desire burned in his belly.

Somehow, he made it to the door. A series of warning growls issued from under the trailer when he pushed it open.

"I'll see you tomorrow."

Lissa waited until the door had closed behind him to slump back against the wall, as boneless as a bowl of Jell-O and twice as shaky.

"Not if I see you first, Counselor."

Chapter 6

Lissa opened the trailer door just as dawn spiraled across the eastern horizon. Great pinwheels of red and gold soothed her gritty eyes. Clean desert air not yet heated to a sizzle by the sun filled her lungs.

She had to get some exercise, had to clear her mind. Evan Henderson had destroyed her concentration and sabotaged any hope of finishing the lyrics she'd been working on when he came visiting last night. The memory of those insane moments when she'd ached for his kiss had kept her tossing and turning for hours. As soon as the first fingers of dawn had slipped through the blinds, she'd rolled out of bed and tugged on her trusty cotton/

spandex sports bra, a comfortable top and her favorite cutoffs.

A long run was exactly what she needed to
sweep the confusion he'd generated from her mind.
A very long run. Hopefully Charlie would have his
bike fixed and the man would be on his way back
to San Diego by the time she got back.

With the ease of long practice, she started slow
and worked her way up to a comfortable jog. The
rhythm of the run helped soothe her jangly nerves.
So did the familiar slap of her sneakers against
hard-baked earth as she followed her favorite path
along the top of the ridge. She kept a wary eye out
for any snakes that might be slithering about their
business in the cool dawn. She'd made it a point
to bone up on the local wildlife when she'd first
moved to Paradise. All the articles she'd read indicated the rattlers indigenous to this corner of the
desert were defensive animals, more likely to
scurry away when startled than attack. Lissa wasn't
anxious to test that particular theory.

Thankfully nothing disturbed the still, stark
landscape except the occasional hawk dive-bomb-
ing for prey. The sky lightened to a hazy blue
above her. Below the ridge she ran along, the desert stretched like a rumpled carpet for miles in
every direction. Night-blooming cacti displayed
splashes of their summer whites and pinks and reds
in the cool dawn.

For all its seeming desolation, Lissa had come to love this vast, untamed land. Her worries faded into insignificance in the face of such awesome, empty splendor. She might have been alone in the world except for Wolf. He loped ahead of her, dodging cactus clumps and sniffing out rabbit holes. Twice, he streaked after unseen prey. Once, he disappeared for a good ten minutes, only to return with tongue lolling and a silly grin on his face that was far more playful dog than half-wild beast.

After four miles, Lissa's common sense had asserted itself. After five, she'd put her crazy urge to lift her mouth to Evan's last night in perspective. She was a normal, healthy female. It wasn't a sin to feel the kind of needs Evan stirred in her.

Only to give in to them.

Well, she hadn't given in to to them last night and wouldn't have to worry about them today. After the way she'd turned down flat both his help and his kiss, Henderson wouldn't offer either again. He'd roar out of Paradise on that bike of his without a backward glance, aim it straight south and head back to his busy life and whoever waited for him in San Diego. A man like Evan Henderson would have someone waiting. Telling herself that was exactly the way she wanted things, she whistled for Wolf and turned to retrace her steps.

The sun was spitting bright, dazzling rays across the sky by the time the trailer came into sight. Slick with sweat, Lissa rounded the end and came to a skidding, clumsy stop.

The calm she'd just pumped into her system went up in a flash of surprise, dismay, and secret, silly delight at finding Evan camped on the trailer steps, eyeing the growling Wolf warily. Disgusted by her reaction, she planted her fists on her hips.

"What are you doing here?"

"Waiting for you."

When he wrapped his hands around two cardboard cups and pushed off the steps, Lissa tried her darnedest to convince herself that the thump inside her heaving chest was merely the result of exertion.

Evan was too busy keeping a cautious eye on Wolf's yellowed fangs to notice much of Lissa's reaction to his presence on her doorstep. He walked forward slowly, keeping his movements calm and unthreatening. To his relief, he made it past the bristling animal without losing a chunk of his flesh. That obstacle cleared, he faced the equally bristling female.

"I brought you some coffee."

Her mouth pursed. She regarded the cup he held out with the same suspicion she'd regarded his offer of help last night.

How the heck she could pucker up like a drying prune and still look so damned sexy escaped Evan. But then, a lot about this woman escaped him. Like how the hurt she tried so hard to disguise with cynicism had kept him awake for most of the night. And how a silvery drop of perspiration trickling down the hollow between her breasts could get him so damned aroused so fast.

Since Lissa had picked him up yesterday afternoon, Evan had gained a whole new appreciation for the sun culture…particularly when it resulted in curling, sweat-dampened hair, flushed skin and cutoffs that displayed to perfection her trim, slender thighs. With an exercise of sheer will, he managed to keep his bland gaze aimed at her face.

"Josephine said you take your coffee with lots of cream. She also said you're partial to spice cake. She sent some along with her, uh, egg bake. I'm not sure what's in it exactly, but it sure smelled good when she pulled it out of the oven a while ago."

It still smelled good, as evidenced by the dog's sudden interest in the paper sack Evan had left on the trailer steps.

"Wolf! Down!"

Tucking his tail between his hind legs, the shaggy creature abandoned the bag and slunk under the trailer. Evan watched with considerable interest as remorse instantly chased the lingering suspicion from Lissa's face.

"Poor baby. He's hungry."

So was Evan. He swallowed an instinctive protest as she fished a foil-covered dish out of the sack and proceeded to empty half its contents into a plastic bowl. Charlie's armadillo stew had wreaked almost as much havoc on Evan's stomach last night as Lissa had on his peace of mind. He'd been salivating ever since Josephine pulled that steaming concoction out of the oven this morning.

He hadn't questioned her sly expression when she'd asked him to carry the dish up to the trailer to share with Lissa. Hard-nosed prosecutor that he was, even Evan shied away from grilling a woman about her motives when she was decked out in flamingo pink baby doll pajamas, yellow plastic hair rollers the size of orange juice cans and rhinestone cat glasses.

The saliva he'd swallowed in Josephine's kitchen, however, didn't compare to the rush that wet his throat when Lissa went down on one knee. Placing the bowl on the flat rocks laid out to form a rectangular patio of sorts, she bent over to coax the animal from its lair.

Her shorts stretched taut across her bottom. The waistband tugged down, separating from her T-shirt. The ragged hems inched up, revealing the sweet, tantalizing curve of her rear cheeks. Evan didn't even *think* about looking away.

To his intense disappointment, Wolf required only a minimum of coaxing. Flashing a warning glance at the strange male invading his territory, the dog emerged from the shadows under the trailer and attacked the bowl's contents.

Lissa watched him gobble down the goodies with some satisfaction, then swiveled around on her heel just in time to catch Evan's wry expression.

"Oh! Was that supposed to be your breakfast or mine?"

"Both."

"Well," she conceded with something less than graciousness, "there's still some left."

"I'm willing to share if you are."

Since he'd toted the stuff up the hill, she could hardly refuse. The prospect of sitting across from him at a breakfast table obviously didn't thrill her, though. Frowning, she started to rise.

Instinctively Evan reached down a hand to help her up. She hesitated for a second, maybe two. When her fingers touched his, a ridiculous sense of victory curled in his stomach. Gently he tugged her to her feet. The scent of her filled his nostrils. Sun-warmed and dusty, with a touch of the desert in her damp, curling hair.

"Thanks," she muttered, retrieving the remaining casserole before she reached for the door. It opened easily at her touch. "I'll wash up. Then we'll eat."

"Don't you lock your door?" Evan asked as he followed her inside, cardboard cups in hand.

"Not usually."

His urban instincts sent up an immediate red flag. "You should, even here in Paradise."

"Yes," she murmured. "I probably should."

She disappeared down a narrow hallway that

led, presumably, to the bedroom and bath. A sliding door bumped across a track to close behind her.

Evan deposited the coffee cups on the chipped
Formica counter and hooked his thumbs in his
jeans pockets. Last night Lissa had absorbed him
so much he'd registered only a few peripheral im-
pressions of the dilapidated tin box she called
home. Today, she absorbed him even more, but
what he'd learned from his early-morning call to
his assistant caused him to look around with a new
eye.

Nothing in Lissa's trailer tracked with Sharon's
crisp, detailed report. According to the information
she'd gathered, Melissa Marie James, aka Missy
Marie, had amassed millions during her meteoric
rise from gospel prodigy to country superstar. In
the process, she'd acquired a taste for the good life.
Her credit reports showed a history of spending
that would have drained the gold reserves at Fort
Knox. It had certainly far outstripped her eight-
figure yearly income.

A good portion of the money, Sharon reported,
had gone to worthy causes. A children's home in
Oklahoma had received a two-million-dollar infu-
sion of cash and new furnishings. Just about any
church that applied to the singer for donations had
come away with far more than they asked for.
She'd also contributed the funds for a new wing at
the Dallas Children's Hospital.

The bubble eventually burst when federal investigators started looking into a series of scams to milk even more money from her legions of fans. Her manager had been named as a codefendant in the resulting indictment, but skipped the country before the case came to trial. Melissa Marie James took the heat alone.

After her trial, the horse farm outside Nashville, the Jaguar and Mercedes SUV, the gaudy, diamond-heeled cowboy boots and jeweled hatbands had all been sold to pay off creditors and those taken in by the scam. The forced sales hadn't generated nearly enough to recoup all the victims' losses. They'd been repaid gradually over the past three years, Sharon reported. A few more each month. The list maintained by the Nashville D.A.'s office had now dwindled to only a handful of names.

That correlated to Lissa's angry assertion last night that she'd paid back almost every penny. Looking around the tiny trailer, Evan wondered how. She claimed she didn't know where her absent manager had disappeared to, along with the bulk of the stolen funds. To repay the debts piled up in her name, she had to have generated considerable income herself these past three years.

If so, she certainly didn't spend it on herself. That pickup she tooled around in should have been junked years ago. And this place…

The furniture must have come with the trailer. The coffee table and lumpy, square-backed sofa

had a definite sixties look. The cheap pecan lami-
nate on the wall paneling had peeled away in some
spots, darkened to almost black in others. From
what Evan could see of the kitchen, it had been
equipped well before the advent of dishwashers or
trash compactors.

Yet surprisingly, the place didn't feel tired or
depressed. Maybe because of the cheerful yellow
scarves draped like swags over the windows. Or
the profusion of wild daisies sprouting from the
blue teapot sitting next to the keyboard.

Evan's gaze snagged on the stack of sheet music
anchored by the teapot. The vehemence of Lissa's
denial when he'd asked if she'd composed the song
he'd heard her singing last night had been all out
of proportion to the question.

He threw a thoughtful glance at the sliding door.
From behind the thin panel came the sound of
splashing water. Casually Evan ambled over to the
table. To his disappointment, the sheets lay face-
down.

Curiosity dug at him like a roweled spur. He
reached out a hand, then slowly pulled it back.
Much as he wanted to, he couldn't bring himself
invade Lissa's privacy.

He was waiting in the trailer's only armchair
when she emerged a few moments later, scrubbed,
combed and, regrettably, wearing another long,
filmy skirt. Evan had developed a decided fondness
for those ragged cutoffs.

Not that there was anything wrong with her swirly lavender-and-green flowered skirt and demure little purple sleeveless top. She'd pulled her hair back in a loose twist and clamped it to her head with one of those plastic thingies, but enough tendrils escaped to frame her cheeks with the same silky softness her feathery bangs framed her eyes.

She looked, he decided with a hitch in his pulse, like a spring morning in a high mountain meadow. Fresh and clean and so *un*like the mascaraed and spangled superstar sex kitten that Evan stopped kicking himself for not having made the connection.

"I'll pop what's left of the casserole in the oven to warm it up," she said stiffly. "Would you like some fresh coffee?"

"I'd love some. I'll make it if you'll tell me where the fixings are."

"Thanks, but there's only room for one person to maneuver in this kitchen. I'll do it."

She ducked down to put a match to the pilot light on the ancient gas stove. After a long series of snapping clicks, the burner caught with a whoosh. That done, she filled a glass carafe and tipped water from it into a coffeemaker. Her movements were smooth and economical, her face a study in concentration and a watchful wariness that told Evan she wasn't at all comfortable with his presence.

He stretched out, enjoying the unusual pleasure

of watching a woman at work in the kitchen. His
mother had insisted that her big, noisy brood know
to cook as well as clean up after themselves. His
brothers had all married women who expected their
mates to spend as much or more time at the stove
as they did. Evan himself could whip up a mean
Caesar salad and marinated steak when the urge
moved him. Given his long hours and grinding
schedule, it didn't move him very often.

His reluctant hostess picked at her eggs after she
put two plates on the table. Evan downed his with
the same gusto Wolf had, then moved on to the
spice cake. He was on his second piece when Lissa
stopped pushing the crumbs around her plate and
met his gaze.

"Why did you come up here this morning? I
told you last night I don't want or need your help."

"The not wanting part came through loud and
clear. The not needing part kept me awake for a
long time after I left you."

That wasn't all that had kept him awake, but she
didn't need to know that now.

"I have a lot of resources at my disposal. If
you'll tell me what got you so spooked in La-
Grange, maybe I can nose around, run some
checks. Some *careful* checks," he added to fore-
stall the protest he saw forming in her eyes.

"There's nothing to check. It was just a weird,
itchy feeling. Nothing I could pinpoint."

He might have believed her if her fork hadn't tapped a nervous beat against her plate.

"And?"

The fork pinged a few more times.

"And I spotted a car parked outside Paradise a couple of times," she said slowly, reluctantly. "Early in the morning, when I run. I wasn't close enough to get its make or see if anyone was inside, and it was gone when I made the return trip."

Evan sensed she was holding back, not yet ready or willing to trust him. Wrapping his hands around his coffee mug, he prompted again.

"And?"

The fork stilled. Lissa lifted her head, met his steady gaze.

"And I think someone opened my mail."

His federal prosecutor's antenna shot straight up. "What makes you think that?"

"I have all my correspondence sent to Mrs. McNabb…a friend of mine back in Oklahoma. She bundles it up and forwards it to me here in Paradise."

So that's how she'd managed to preserve her privacy for so long. Simple, but effective.

"One of the envelopes she forwarded a month or so ago had been opened. Mrs. McNabb put a note on it, saying she'd found it in her mailbox like that."

"Tampering with the mail is a federal offense. Did you report it?"

Her mouth twisted. "What do you think?"

He brushed aside her obvious reluctance to land herself in the middle of another mail fraud investigation, even as a potential victim.

"What was in the envelope?"

Lissa chewed on her lower lip. For a long moment, the only sound in the trailer was the faint rattle of the butane-fed swamp cooler that pushed damp air through the vents.

They'd reached a critical point, Evan realized. For him to help her, she had to take a step she obviously didn't want to make. He leaned forward, wondering why the heck he was so determined to forge a bond of trust between them. He'd be out of here in a few hours, on his way back to San Diego by midafternoon at the latest.

"If I was going to breach your confidence, I could have done so yesterday when the reporter came nosing around," he reminded her quietly. "You can tell me what was in the envelope."

Blowing out a long breath, she laid aside the fork. "A contract from a music publisher. I write and sell gospel songs under a pseudonym."

"Like 'One-Way Ticket to Paradise'?"

"Yes." A flush crept up her neck. "I didn't actually lie last night when you asked if I'd composed that hymn. It's, uh, still in the works."

He let that bit of truth-stretching slide. "I didn't catch the words, but what I heard of the melody was beautiful."

"Thanks."

"Are you writing both the music and the lyrics? For some reason, I thought those were two different specialties."

"Most of the time they are. I've always done both."

Her face softened, giving it a sweetness that made his breath hitch.

"The McNabbs bought me an accordion when I was a kid. I spent some of the happiest years of my life pumping out tunes and singing silly verses to go with them." Kinder memories than those she'd stored up in the past few years filled her eyes. "Eventually I graduated to a guitar, then a keyboard, but I still have a soft spot in my heart for that old squeeze box."

The urge to keep her talking pulled at Evan. Without the sharp edge of wariness, her voice flowed over him like warm wine.

"You mentioned the McNabbs a couple of times. They sound like good people."

"They are. They raised me from the time I was four."

"What happened to your folks?"

"My mother died in a car accident. My father..." One shoulder lifted in a careless shrug. "He disappeared a year later."

Pity tugged at Evan, but Lissa's soft, private smile as she described the couple who raised her showed she wasn't looking for either pity or sympathy.

"The McNabbs gave me all the love any child could need. They taught me to rejoice in the Lord and in my music. I stayed with them until I was sixteen."

Until Jonah "Doc" Dawes appeared on the scene.

Sharon's report on the agent who'd taken charge of Missy Marie's career had been brief and to the point. The promoter had struck gold in the naive, trusting young singer and mined it for all it was worth. All during his stint as her manager, Dawes had cut himself in for an incredible fifty percent of his client's gross income as his commission. He'd also dressed her in enough spangles to outfit a Broadway chorus line and, according to Hollywood's inveterate gossip columnists, eventually became far more than her business partner.

Evan's gut twisted at the thought. No wonder Lissa carried her wariness like a barbed shield. First, her father abandoned her. Then a sleazy Svengali had breezed into her life and seduced her. Now...

Now, a slick assistant district attorney had landed in Paradise and was trying to do the same damned thing.

Abruptly Evan pushed away from the table. "I'll tell you what. I've got a little time before Charlie finishes my bike. I'll borrow his truck and drive back to LaGrange. Nose around a bit. See if I can find a clue to what spooked you yesterday.''

Lissa scrambled up. "You don't have to do that.''

"I know I don't have to. I want to. I'll be back in a couple of hours."

"Don't you need to get home?" she asked stiffly.

With a careless grin, Evan dismissed the combined demands for his immediate return by his boss, his assistant, and an increasingly impatient Carrie Northcutt.

"I'll head out for San Diego later this afternoon."

Chapter 7

Lissa almost let him make the drive into La-Grange by himself. She hadn't asked him to chase down whatever had given her that uneasy feeling. Hadn't asked for his help at all.

Scowling, she watched him stride halfway down the hill before common sense kicked in. The last thing she needed was an assistant D.A. asking questions about her and stirring curiosity in town. Flinging open the trailer door, she rushed after him.

"Evan! Wait!"

His mirrored sunglasses caught the glare and threw it back at her. A moment later, Lissa caught up with him.

"You're a stranger around these parts. You'll get more questions than answers in LaGrange."

The corners of his mouth kicked up. "I've had some experience at drawing information out of folks without being too obvious."

"If you say so." Her doubting tone pulled a full grin from Evan. "Look, I appreciate that you're only trying to help, but…"

"Come with me."

"Excuse me?"

"Drive into LaGrange with me. That way you can show me the town and I can watch people's reactions to you while we ask our questions."

The idea of spending any more time with him again didn't appear to appeal to her. She shook her head, backpedaling fast.

"Let's just drop the whole idea. You've got better things to do than wander around a hot, dusty town on a Saturday morning."

"None that I can think of," he said with cheerful untruth. "We might as well take your pickup. Get your keys and some sunglasses and we'll hit the road."

How did he do it? Lissa wondered two hours later. How the heck did he walk up to perfect strangers and charm them into long conversations?

His first target had been the minister at the Christian Evangelical Church where they'd stopped on the pretext of inquiring whether Lissa was needed to fill in as organist at tomorrow's services. Then the pimple-faced kid leaning against his car fender outside on the street. Now the waitress at the Dairy Freeze where they'd dropped in for something cold.

Lissa recognized Jill Jefferson from church and from her infrequent visits into town, but the waitress had never acted quite this friendly before. Or this flirty. Propping a hip against the edge of their circular booth, the bubbly brunette took advantage of a lull between customers to ask how their root beer freezes were going down.

"Like snow sliding off a polar bear's back," Evan replied with a twinkle in his eyes.

Jill's smile could have melted the ice cap. "We aim to please, cowboy. I haven't seen you around here before, have I?"

"I doubt it," he answered easily if somewhat evasively. "I'm from up around Flagstaff. I don't travel this way often."

"Too bad." Her curious glance flicked between the two occupants of the booth. "So are you and Lissa old friends or what?"

"More like new friends."

Ignoring the loud gurgle when Lissa's straw sucked air from the bottom of her mug, Evan stretched an arm across the back of the booth and kept the waitress talking.

"She's been showing me around LaGrange. Nice town you've got here."

"Yeah," Jill snorted. "What there is of it."

The buckshot-peppered sign on the outskirts had pegged LaGrange's population at four hundred and forty-nine. Not exactly a thriving metropolis, although it was definitely uptown compared to Paradise.

Laid out in a flat grid with scraggly trees shading its center and cactus sprouting just about everywhere else, the town boasted an elementary school, a post office, a bank, two churches, three beer joints and a video rental/convenience store around the corner from the Dairy Freeze. For more esoteric delights like Wal-Marts or McDonald's, the residents traveled to Buckeye, an hour to the north, or to Yuma, an hour and a half to the south.

"What do folks do for fun around here on a Saturday?" Evan asked casually.

Just as casually, his finger stroked the bare skin of Lissa's shoulder. Her nerves flickered like fireflies at the light touch. With considerable restraint, she managed not to jerk away.

She sat silent while Evan skillfully extracted more information from the chatty waitress. Within moments, he'd learned that Jasper's Pool Hall constituted LaGrange's social center, the latest titles in the video store next door, the occupation and approximate income of the town's wealthiest citizens, and the name of the county sheriff whose nine thousand-square-mile jurisdiction included LaGrange township.

"His office is up to the county seat," Jill volunteered, "but one of Sheriff Lester's deputies lives right here in town."

The sheriff's name must have meant something to Evan, as his hand stilled for a second or two before resuming its maddening stroke.

"That must have been the deputy's squad car I saw parked outside the pool hall," he commented idly.

"Probably. Art swears he learns just about everything he needs to know about the doings of the town by listening to those boys at the Jasper's."

The entrance of a couple of kids drew the waitress's attention. Thankfully she moved off before the rough feathering of Evan's fingertips had Lissa crawling out of her skin. Edging away, she fired him an irate look.

"Did you have to rub my shoulder like that?"

His grin slipped back into place. "No."

"Then what was the purpose of that charade?"

"Just adding a little local color."

As if he needed any color, local or otherwise, she thought in annoyance. He'd left his San Diego Padres ball cap in the pickup, rolled up the sleeves of his blue cotton shirt and tucked his aviator sunglasses into his pocket. With his tanned skin, snug jeans and scuffed boots comfortably crossed at the ankle, he looked right at home in this dusty little town.

"We've still got a few streets to stroll down, but

I haven't noticed anyone watching you oddly. Any recurrence of that prickly sensation you described?''

Other than the shivers he'd roused all along her spine, Lissa hadn't felt anything but the suffocating heat.

"No. Do you know this sheriff Jill mentioned?" she asked, curious about the way his fingers had stilled at the mention of the man's name.

"Bill Lester? I know *of* him. He used to be with the DEA. My brother Marsh worked a few undercover operations with him before he quit federal service to run for sheriff. Since then, he's made quite a name for himself in law enforcement circles.''

Not just in law enforcement circles. He'd also made the front cover of several national magazines for his controversial, get-tough policy toward crime and criminals. As isolated as she was in Paradise, even Lissa had heard how the sheriff put convicted felons onto chain gangs and housed them in crude tent cities with few amenities instead of in air-conditioned cells. Apparently he believed crime shouldn't pay.

Her own close brush with the law had left too many raw scars for Lissa to feel at all comfortable discussing the pros and cons of such a hard stand. She felt even less comfortable when Evan suggested they walk the block or so to Jasper's Pool Hall and see if the deputy sheriff was in residence.

Hot, sticky and sorry she'd ever involved Evan in her problems, she shook her head. "We're wasting our time here. I'm ready to head back to Paradise."

"I think it might be worth our while to talk to the deputy."

"I'd rather not."

He might recognize her, or wonder why a resident of sleepy little Paradise had hooked up with a deputy U.S. district attorney. Not that Evan had identified himself as such, but Lissa suspected law enforcement officials picked up on other's vibes much as musicians or singers did.

Scooting out of the booth, she untangled her long skirt from around her knees and made for the door. Evan followed her into the lung-searing heat. Once outside, he caught her elbow.

"Give me fifteen minutes to talk to the deputy. Then we'll head back."

The long breath she blew out lifted her bangs. "All right. Fifteen minutes. I'll check the mail at the post office and fill up the truck."

Evan didn't make the mistake of offering to pay for the gas. He'd learned that lesson the hard way. Sliding on his sunglasses, he watched her cross the street to the rusty white pickup. Heat shimmered above the asphalt and enveloped her in iridescent waves. She moved like a dancer through the illusion of silver. Her mint-colored sleeveless top and thin, breezy skirt somehow managed to look cool despite the broiling sun.

She was getting to him. The more time he spent in her company, the more time he *wanted* to spend. Searching his mind for ways to spin out their excursion into LaGrange, he made his way to Jasper's.

He found the deputy sheriff comfortably ensconced on a high stool, elbows bent back against a pine bar blackened by age and hard use. Although his bulging stomach suggested that he overindulged regularly at mealtime, the fact that he held a glass of iced tea in his hand instead of a beer met with Evan's instant approval.

Ordering the same, he claimed a stool a few removed from the man whose name tag identified him as Art Ortega and surveyed the room. Pool balls clacked on the felt-covered table. Smoke spiraled from cigarettes stuck to the players' lower lips. The TV perched precariously on a high shelf in one corner showed flashes of color as stock cars roared around a track.

It was a man's place, similar in decor and sweaty aroma to the pool hall where the Henderson brothers had learned to drop a ball in a corner pocket with a two-rim side shot and swap exaggerated tales of their various exploits with the ranch hands who frequented the joint. Evan felt right at home. Although conscious of the ticking clock, he stayed loose. Small town curiosity and the deputy's instinctive once-over of a stranger in his territory did the trick soon enough.

"Don't think I've seen you around LaGrange before," Ortega commented.

"I passed through yesterday and had some bike trouble about ten miles south of here." Evan downed a long swallow of presweetened tea. "I'm just killing time until my Harley's fixed."

"Who's doing the work?"

"Charlie Haines, down in Paradise."

"Charlie's a good man. If he says he can fix whatever ails your bike, he can." The deputy's gaze roamed over Evan. "If your Harley's in Paradise, how'd you get back to LaGrange."

"I drove up with Lissa James."

Interest gleamed in Ortega's dark eyes. "Isn't she the sweet-looking blonde who plays the organ over at the Evangelical Church on the days Avis Thornton's arthritis acts up?"

"That's her," Evan said easily.

From the idle conversation that followed, he was soon convinced that the deputy hadn't connected sweet-looking Lissa James with hot-looking, one-time singing sensation Missy Marie. And if Art Ortega, Jill Jefferson and the pastor of the Christian Evangelical Church hadn't made the leap, it was a pretty good bet that no one else in LaGrange had, either.

Reassured for Lissa's sake yet disappointed that he hadn't been able to pin down the source of her uneasiness, Evan left Jasper's a few minutes later. A quick sweep down the street showed the pickup parked beside a gas pump at the convenience store. Hot and flushed, Lissa fretted with the nozzle.

Evan reached the parking lot just as a grizzled attendant emerged from the store.

"I'll do that for you, miss. That pump gets ornery sometimes."

Sweeping her hair back with a palm, Lissa gave him one of the smiles she rationed out so meagerly to Evan. "Thanks."

She turned away then, missing the intent look the store clerk gave her in return. Missing, too, the way his gaze followed her through the cloud of heat and fuel fumes oscillating above the pickup's gas tank.

Evan's senses jumped to full alert. He crossed the street at a quick lope, but when he got close enough to see through the fumes distorting the attendant's lean, gray-whiskered features, he found them curiously blanked. He made a mental note of the man's age—late forties, he guessed—and the employee ID tag on his green striped shirt. "Arlen" could be either his first or last name. Neither one would be that difficult to run down when combined with his general description and the tattoo of an eagle peeking out from under his shirtsleeve.

"I'll be right back," Evan told Lissa as she handed the attendant a ten-dollar bill and climbed behind the wheel of the pickup. "I just want to get something cold and wet for the trip back to Paradise.''

In addition to cold and wet, the cardboard container he carried out of the store a few minutes later also held a paper bag that oozed hot and spicy scents. More importantly, his wallet contained a scrap of paper with the phone number of the store scribbled across it. He might just need to talk to the clerk's supervisor.

"What's that?" Lissa asked, eyeing the paper bag suspiciously.

"Lunch."

"Didn't we just eat breakfast a couple of hours ago, with a root beer freeze on top of that?"

"We did, but I was hoping to convince you to detour by Painted Rocks Dam on the way back to Paradise."

Frowning, she keyed the ignition and elbowed the truck into gear. "That's a good thirty miles out of the way."

"I know. That's why I picked up lunch."

Hot wind dived in through open windows and lifted the ends of her hair as they left the outskirts of LaGrange and picked up speed.

"Why the sudden interest in a dam?"

"It's not all that sudden. My brother Reece worked a major redesign of the intake tower a few years ago. I've been wanting to see his handiwork."

Evan saw no reason to let drop that he'd man-

aged to contain his desire to see Reece's handiwork until this afternoon.

"How many brothers do you have?" she asked,
tilting him a curious glance.

"Four."

"Older or younger?"

"Both. I'm second in line. Jake's the oldest,
then me, then Marsh…"

"He's the DEA agent."

Surprised she'd remembered, Evan nodded.
"Right. Then there's Reece, an engineer with the
Bureau of Reclamation, and Sam, the youngest.
Normally he pilots Air Force test aircraft, but right
now he's flying a desk in Washington and isn't too
happy about it."

"A pilot, an engineer, an undercover agent and
an attorney. Busy bunch, you Hendersons. What
does Jake do?"

"He runs the Bar-H, the ranch we grew up on.
We all own shares in the operation and get home
as often as we can to help out, but Jake's the one
with his boots planted deep in the rangeland."

Propping an elbow on the open window, Lissa
twisted a strand of fluttering hair around a finger.
"No female Hendersons to counteract all that tes-
tosterone?"

"No sisters, if that's what you mean, but my
brothers have all had rings put through their noses.
I've collected a whole passle of sisters-in-law over
the years." He hesitated before adding, "I lost one,

too. Jake's wife, Ellen, was killed in a drive-by shooting six months ago.''

''Oh, no!'' Shocked, she pulled her gaze from the road. ''How awful! I'm so sorry for your brother.''

''Me, too,'' Evan said simply.

They were quiet for a while, each retreating into their own thoughts. Evan's gut still twisted whenever he remembered shy, elfin Ellen. He'd loved her like a sister, yet knew his aching sense of loss couldn't come anywhere close to the pain that ravaged Jake.

Like Lissa, Jake had pulled away from the rest of the world. He was slowly burying himself in Jack Daniel's instead of hiding out in a ghost town in the middle of the desert, but the result was the same. And like Lissa, Jake didn't particularly want Evan bulldozing his way into his self-styled retreat.

Tough. He'd planted himself feetfirst in the middle of Jake's problem and landed on his butt in the middle of Lissa's. He wasn't giving up either one until he'd done whatever he could to help.

''What about you?'' she asked, breaking into his thoughts. ''Why hasn't some woman put a ring through your nose, too?''

''A couple have come pretty close, but I managed to get away with a whole hide.''

His smug male satisfaction had her shaking her head. ''Your time will come, Henderson.''

And soon, Evan thought wryly, if Carrie Northcutt had her way. As the wind whipped through the open windows and his gaze lingered on Lissa's profile, realization settled in his gut. He had to make it clear to Carrie that the incident on the conference table in his office wasn't going to happen again.

Although he admired her legal skills and respected her ambition, Evan knew he'd never love her. Hell, he'd worked with her for three months now and hadn't experienced anything close to the frustrating combination of lust and fascination Lissa had roused in a mere twenty-four hours.

He'd tell Carrie when he got back to San Diego, he vowed silently. She deserved to know things weren't going anywhere between them. Deserved more than he could give her, although Evan knew she saw him as much as a means to an end as a potential bed partner. She intended to make her mark within the Justice Department with the Mendoza case.

Deliberately he pushed both Mendoza and Carrie Northcutt from his mind. He'd face both of them soon enough. For the next few hours, at least, he'd concentrate on Lissa.

It didn't take much effort. She was eminently concentrate-able. By the time they turned onto the narrow, twisting dirt road that led to Painted Rocks Dam, Evan had memorized the clean line of her chin and throat. Memorized, too, the way her mouth pursed when she fought to contain a smile.

He was getting better at pulling them out of her. He'd won one with his smug reference to his narrow matrimonial escapes. He coaxed another with his suggestion that they take their sack lunch down to the sandy, rock-strewn edge of the reservoir behind the dam for a picnic.

Lissa studied the barren landscape beside the trapped waters of the Gila River. Aside from several clumps of prickly pear and a tall, spiky century plant that thrust its stalk a good ten or twelve feet into the air, there wasn't a patch of green to be seen.

"You want to picnic here?" she asked with a lift of one brow. "It's probably a hundred degrees plus out in that sun."

"If we get too hot, we can always strip off and go skinny-dipping."

The hopeful note in his voice drew a grin. "In your dreams, Henderson."

She's got that right, Evan thought as they climbed out of the pickup and he followed her down to the water's edge. The sight of Lissa James kicking off a sandal and lifting her skirt to test the water with her toes would figure in his dreams for a long time to come.

Sunlight streamed through the flowered material, silhouetting her slender legs. The same dazzling light tinted her tanned skin to a deep gold and made a glowing nimbus of her hair. And when she jerked her toes from the dark water, laughing in surprised delight at its icy chill, Evan's lust took a sharp turn into something he couldn't quite define.

Chapter 8

Whenever she looked back at the stolen hour beside the Painted Rocks Dam, Lissa was always amazed at the sheer pleasure two people could derive from soggy burritos, warm soft drinks and the utterly mistaken belief they might bridge the vast differences separating them.

With the sun almost directly overhead, there wasn't much shade to be found. The only relief was at the very base of the tower fifty or so yards from the massive, earth-filled structure that stretched between arid hills. Sliding one hand under Lissa's elbow and balancing the cardboard food contained in the other, Evan guided her over the rocks to the miserly slice of shade projected by the tower. Gratefully she hiked up her skirt and sank down at the edge of its concrete platform, dangling her feet over the side. The cool water tickled her toes.

Evan, she admitted on an inner sigh when he pulled off his boots and socks and dropped his feet into the water beside hers, tickled everything else. Her senses worked overtime, cataloging everything from the tingly brush of his arm against hers as he made himself comfortable to the strong, masculine scent of his sun-warmed skin.

"Reece built this tower," he told her, his voice echoing with quiet pride. "The original intake couldn't handle the Upper Colorado's floods of '92. The Bureau of Reclamation brought him back from a UN project in Africa to head the emergency reconstruction and repair team."

Craning her neck, Lissa peered upward. The tower stood tall and ramrod straight, like a sentry at Buckingham Palace. Its concrete gleamed a cleaner white than the weathered face of the dam.

"What, exactly, does an intake tower do?"

"Reece could give you the technical explanation, but essentially, it sucks water from the reservoir and deposits it on the other side of the dam. If the reservoir rises too high because of heavy rains or snow melt upriver, the intake opens wider to prevent flooding."

Jamming a straw into one of the super giant-size soft drinks, he offered it to Lissa. She sipped the warm contents contentedly while he peeled the paper off a second straw.

She couldn't believe how relaxed she felt...and curious. The bits Evan had told her about his brothers had subtly altered her mental mosaic of the man beside her. Made him seem more real somehow. More three-dimensional.

More than just a lazy grin and a pair of sexy blue eyes, anyway.

Setting aside her drink, she drew up one leg and wrapped her arms around her knee. Her chin found a comfortable prop on the bony shelf. "Tell me about this ranch you grew up on."

"The Bar-H?" He angled around to lean a shoulder against the concrete wall behind him. "The Bar-H is twenty thousand prime acres nestled at the base of the San Francisco peaks. Summers, the cattle graze high meadows thick with the sweetest grass this side of the Rockies. Winters, we bring them down below the pine belt to lower ranges sheltered by the mountains."

"It sounds like beautiful country."

"It is. It can also be brutal. I've spent more hours than I care to remember with Sam at the controls of our twin-engine Commanche, flying through blizzards to air-drop hay to near frozen cattle."

"Do you ever regret leaving the Bar-H to practice law?"

"All the time." The skin at the corners of his

eyes crinkled. "Especially when I'm up to my, uh, ears in dope runners and embezzlers."

That last cut too close to Lissa's own past for comfort. Her gaze dropped to the water swirling around her foot.

"What about you?" he asked quietly. "Do you ever regret leaving the recording studios and the bright stage lights behind?"

"No, never."

She drew a circle in the water with her big toe, watching the ripples weave a pattern from the base of the tower. Evan didn't press, which was probably why she opened up. Slowly. Cautiously. Dragging out memories that could still make her writhe with embarrassment at her incredible stupidity.

"I admit I loved it at first. The first year or so, I was still singing the songs I'd learned as a child. It thrilled me that people would want to hear messages of faith and joy. Every time I stepped out on the stage or clamped on a set of earphones in a recording booth, I'd shiver with the sheer magic of it all."

The ripples she'd stirred widened, flattened, gradually disappeared on the placid surface of the reservoir.

"What happened to the magic?"

"The business end of things sort of swallowed it up. The audiences kept growing and CD sales went crazy and Doc..."

Lissa caught her lower lip between her teeth. She couldn't blame anyone except herself for what happened.

"I changed to fit the spiraling demand. My appearance, my vocal techniques, my backup singers. Even my music."

Especially her music. She could still remember her nervousness when she'd recorded her first crossover CD. Just to test the waters, Doc had said. See if her gospel fans would buy a new sound. They'd bought it, along with millions of country fans.

Seemingly overnight, Missy Marie was the hottest new commodity in the high stakes, multibillion-dollar music entertainment industry. Her public concerts tripled, soon eclipsing and then edging out completely the revivals and church-sponsored singing festivals that had given her such inspiration and joy. In her new persona, she spent three weeks out of every month on the road, slept most of the day after exhausting, four- and five-hour concerts and crammed whatever leftover energy and time she had into recording sessions.

Just about the time Lissa had started questioning whether that was the life she wanted to live, it all fell apart.

"Now I'm writing the songs I love again. I can't ask for anything more. I don't need anything more."

She believed that, Evan realized. She really believed she could insulate herself from the joys and jagged sorrows that constituted life. She'd wrapped herself in isolation and called it peace.

"You don't think there might be a middle ground between Paradise and the hell you went through?" he asked gently.

"If there is, I'm not looking for it."

He didn't miss the defensive note that crept into her voice. He should have backed off then. Left her to her dry, desert sanctuary. He might have done just that if her edgy sense of unease hadn't infected him, too.

He couldn't shake the feeling that her days of solitude were numbered. The hungry reporter Evan had chased off wouldn't give up. If Dave Hawthorne didn't find the fallen star, another one like him would. She was too good a story to give up on.

"It's a shaky proposition, putting your life on hold the way you have."

"I haven't put it on hold," she said with a stubborn tilt to her chin. "I'm happy right where I am, doing exactly what I'm doing."

"Don't you get hungry for someone to talk to or laugh with? Someone who'll get you out of that trailer and into town for a movie or a root beer freeze once in a while?"

"I've got Charlie and Josephine to talk to, and I don't need a steady diet of movies or root beer freezes."

She'd gone all prickly on him again. Evan couldn't resist the challenge of trying to get past those sharp little spikes.

"Tell me the last time you slurped down a freeze before today."

"It's been..." She flapped a hand in annoyance. "A while."

"How long, Lissa? A month? Six months?"

"For heaven's sake, I don't know. What business is it of yours, anyway?"

"I'm just trying to gauge my chances of collecting that Saturday Night Special."

"What!"

"I know it's only Saturday afternoon," he said, grinning at her dumbfounded expression. "But if it's been six months or more since you shared a soda with anyone except Josephine or Charlie, it's probably been about that long since you shared a kiss. I might just get lucky here."

Her mouth sagged. Laughing, Evan leaned forward to curl a knuckle under her chin. He nudged her jaw up, delighting in the flush that heated the skin under his fingers.

"Well?" he teased.

No way Lissa was going to admit her long, dry spell when it came to kisses stretched back almost to the dawn of the nuclear age. Or that his chances of getting lucky increased exponentially every second he grinned down at her with that outrageous, blatantly male glint in his eyes.

Evidently she didn't have to admit anything. Evan must have read the answer in the mulish set to her mouth. Pure devilment danced in his eyes. He leaned closer, until his lips were a whisper from hers.

"What do you say, Lissa? Want to go for it? Mouths open? Teeth knocking?"

She couldn't breathe. The heat suffocated her. The heat, and his confounded nearness. He interpreted her choked silence as consent. Lissa didn't lie to herself. That's just how she'd hoped he'd interpret it.

"Open your mouth, sweetheart. Just a little."

The huskiness in his voice surprised her. Him, too, if the sudden quirk in his brow was any indication. She expected him to draw back then. When he didn't, her heart leapfrogged straight into her throat.

"That's it," he murmured, bending to brush his mouth across hers. "Just like that."

She didn't know her lips had parted. Had no idea her breath was racing in and out until he stopped it with his own.

One kiss, she thought. A few seconds of light contact. That's all it was. All she'd allow it to be.

She hadn't figured he would nudge her chin up another notch and fit his mouth more firmly over hers. That added ten or fifteen seconds more of pure sensation.

The hand he slid around her waist to draw her against him added a few more.

Then his mouth came down on hers, harder, hotter, and Lissa gave up all attempts at timing the contact, much less controlling it. Her arms wrapped around his neck. Her mouth clung to his. Teeth knocked. Tongues tangled.

She felt, she thought while she could still think at all, like a parched wanderer stumbling down a sand dune toward a lush, tropical oasis. Heady with his scent, hungry for his taste, she sampled every delight. Her fingers curled into the hair at his nape. Her ear picked up the tempo of his breathing, as deep and ragged as her own. Her breasts tingled where they crushed against his chest.

For the life of her, Lissa couldn't say whether Evan ended the kiss or she did. All she knew was that the laughter had disappeared from his eyes when he lifted his head. His cheeks flushed under their tan, he stared down at her. A wayward strand of his short beaver-brown hair had fallen forward. Lissa ached to reach up, brush it into place with the other crisp strands. Instead she summoned a smile she sincerely hoped wasn't as wobbly as the darned thing felt.

"Good thing we got that Special out of the way this afternoon…since you'll be leaving Paradise as soon as we get back."

She hadn't framed it as a question, but he answered it anyway. "I have to, Lissa. I've got a case going to the Grand Jury next week. A big case."

Okay. Fine. So what was the big deal here? She'd known from the first moment she'd picked him up that he was just passing through.

"If you plan to make it back to the big city before dark, we'd better get going."

She started to scramble up, but her feet tangled in her skirt at the same time his hand caught her elbow.

"I'll run some inquiries next week. Some *discreet* inquiries," he added when she arched a brow. "Just to see if anyone besides Hawthorne or his buddy has tried to tag your records or ferret out your address."

She'd been on her own so long, it was hard to accept help from anyone. Her head dipped in stiff acknowledgment. "Thanks."

Again, she tried to rise. Again, his warm hand grazed her arm.

"We can't leave yet."

Panic fluttered in her stomach. They sure as dickens couldn't stay here for a repeat of that shattering kiss. She was only human.

"Evan..."

"We haven't had lunch."

The breath she'd just sucked in slid right back out. She'd forgotten the soggy paper sack he'd lugged down with the soft drinks.

"I'm not hungry."

"I am." He hung a suffering expression on his face. "You're not going to send me on my way without sustenance, are you?"

Lissa refused...flatly, absolutely *refused*...to admit that she came perilously close to not wanting to send him on his way at all. Forcing her legs to fold under her, she sank down again.

"What's in the bag?"

"Burritos."

He dug a paper-wrapped tube out of the sack. Rust-colored grease dripped through his fingers and splattered on the concrete.

"Ugh. You're not actually planning to eat that, are you?"

"After Charlie's armadillo stew, I'm game for just about anything. Here, this one's yours."

Laughing, Lissa held up a palm. "No, thanks! I'm still full from Josephine's egg bake and that root beer freeze. They're all yours."

The abandoned bauxite mine outside Paradise came into view at ten past three. Lissa knew the time because she snuck a glance at the no-nonsense black sports watch strapped to Evan's wrist.

Plenty of time for him to make it to Yuma and then on to San Diego before dark. Not that she was worried about him. She just didn't like the idea of a motorcycle whizzing along the interstate at sixty-plus miles an hour, its single taillight lost in the blur of the vehicle traffic that traveled the busy highway.

It didn't even occur to her that he might stay over at Josephine's another night. He had to get back to his work. She had to get back to hers. Yet Lissa couldn't remember the last time she'd driven into Paradise with such mixed emotions. Somehow, her little sanctuary seemed less welcoming and more desolate.

"I'll call you."

His quiet promise drew her gaze from the dilapidated buildings and deserted main street.

"Do you really think you'll turn up anything with these 'discreet' inquires?"

"Maybe, maybe not, but I'll call you in any case."

She nodded, thoroughly uncomfortable with the little shiver of pleasure she derived from the prospect of hearing his voice one more time. She had the rebellious quiver under firm control by the time the native stone gas station/bar came into view.

"You'd better drop me off at Charlie's," Evan said. "I'll check to make sure the bike is ready before I... Oh, hell."

He stiffened suddenly. Lissa shot him a curious glance, then followed his intent stare through the cracked windshield to the cherry-red convertible parked in front of Charlie's Place. Her hands tightened on the wheel.

"Do you think it's Hawthorne?"

"No."

"Maybe he decided to come back in his own car and follow up on his lead."

"It's not Hawthorne."

"How can you be sure?"

"Because I know who owns that car."

"Who?"

"A friend."

Lissa brought the pickup to a stop beside the convertible, wondering at the terse reply. Her confusion cleared a moment later when the screen door banged open.

The woman who emerged wore a short cap of shining black hair, fashionably wrinkled linen shorts and a smile that conveyed both relief and exasperation. Her green eyes zinged to Lissa, then fixed on Evan's tall form as he swung out of the pickup.

"It's about time you showed, Henderson! I've been waiting in this dump for over an hour."

"What are you doing here, Carrie?"

"Sharon told me you were stranded. I came to haul your butt back to San Diego."

"I told her I'd get back when I could."

"'Could' doesn't cut it, Counselor. Not now."

Lissa sat pinned to the sticky plastic seat. Even from inside the pickup's airless cab, she could see the excitement that honed the newcomer's fine-boned features to sharp edges.

"We finally got the break we've been hoping

for. The Chula Vista PD busted one of Mendoza's lieutenants last night on a homicide charge. They caught him with the gun still practically smoking. He wants to cop a plea and testify in exchange for a lesser charge of murder two.''

Obviously electrified by the news, Evan banged the pickup's door shut and whipped off his sunglasses.

''Which lieutenant?''

''Joey Smallwood.''

The feral smile Evan displayed at the news made Lissa gulp. This was a side of him she hadn't seen during their brief acquaintance. Right before her eyes, he'd transformed into a hunter. A legal predator trained to go for the jugular and tear it apart. It was a breed she had more than a passing familiarity with.

''If Smallwood spills even a tenth of what I suspect he knows about Mendoza's operation, we've got him!''

''Why do you think I drove all the way out to this godforsaken excuse for a town to get you? Let's move it, sweet-cakes. We've got a star witness waiting for us.''

Sweet-cakes? Lissa's grip on the wheel tightened another notch.

''I'll check on the Sportster. It should be ready to roll.''

''Send someone for the bike when you get home,'' his friend said impatiently. ''We need to drive back together and talk through the questions we're going to put to Smallwood.''

"Yeah, you're right. I'll let Charlie know.'' He turned to Lissa, sitting stiff and silent. "Hang loose a sec, will you?''

She released her death grip on the steering wheel and reached for the gearshift. "You need to get going. So do I.''

"Just wait here!''

The growled imperative didn't sit well with her, but before she could tell the man to hit the road and take his curt orders with him, he'd disappeared inside Charlie's Place.

Lissa drummed her fingers on the wheel, fighting the urge to shove the truck into gear and drive off. She very much regretted not giving in to the impulse a moment later, when her gaze shifted to the raven-haired woman.

Evan's partner returned Lissa's look with a speculative one of her own. Flawlessly made-up and coolly beautiful despite the brutal heat, she took the initiative and crossed to the truck. Lissa had the feeling she would always take the initiative.

"You must be the Good Samaritan who rescued Evan when he went into the ditch yesterday. Thanks for not leaving him in the desert to bake.''

All too conscious of her windblown hair and the gritty sand in the creases of her skin, Lissa shrugged. "I wouldn't leave anyone stranded like that.''

"Well, I appreciate getting him back in one piece."

"Do you?"

"Yes."

The woman's gaze flicked over her, taking in every dusty detail. If that sweet-cakes bit hadn't already alerted Lissa to what was coming next, her slow, feline smile would have done the trick.

"Just between us girls," she purred, "I didn't wrangle a special detail to work with Henderson on this case solely because of his brilliant mind. Or because he stands a damned good chance of being appointed as the San Diego district's next D.A. The fact is, he's as good in bed as he is in court."

Lissa's stomach twisted, but she wasn't about to let a woman who called Charlie's Place a dump and bragged about her sexual activities in public score points off her.

"Just between us girls," she replied with syrupy sweetness, "he didn't say the same about you."

A tide of red suffused the other woman's cheeks. She started to say something, thought better of it. Whirling, she stalked to her car.

Lissa sat there, biting her lip. Mrs. McNabb would have been shocked to hear her charge utter such a spiteful remark. Lissa might have been a little shocked herself if anger and disgust hadn't crowded out every other emotion.

She'd kissed him! She'd perched on that concrete platform and stared up at him like an idiot, mesmerized by those crinkly laugh lines at the corners of his eyes, waiting—praying—for that kiss to happen. When in heaven's name would she learn!

The bang of the screen door had her gritting her teeth. Evan strode to the truck.

"I'll call you if I stumble across anything you need to know. Even if I don't, I'll call."

"Don't bother, *sweet-cakes.*"

A muscle ticked at the side of his jaw. "I don't have time to explain Carrie to you right now. I'll…"

"You don't owe me any explanations." She shoved the truck into gear. "Besides, she's already made it crystal clear how things stand between you two."

The muscle jumped again. His eyes went flinty but, mercifully, he didn't make the situation worse by dragging it out. Instead he shoved one of his business cards at her.

"I wrote my home phone number on the back. If that itchy sensation starts crawling over you again, call me, okay? Immediately."

Three feet of snow would blanket Paradise first! As anxious now to be rid of him as she was furious with herself for those moments at the dam, Lissa snatched the card from his hand.

"Have a fun trip home."

She left him standing in the dirt outside Charlie's Place. Before she'd driven half a block, she'd torn the card into a dozen pieces and tossed them through the pickup's window.

Chapter 9

Evan banged the receiver down and scowled at the multibutton instrument. Dammit, where was she? Why didn't she answer her phone? He'd been trying off and on to reach her for two days now, ever since he'd received the results of his queries.

His frown sliced deeper as he fingered the manila folder he'd marked with a simple Lissa. Compared to most of the files stacked on his desk, this one was relatively thin. It contained only three sketchy computer-generated reports. One summarized the information Sharon had gathered on Melissa James in response to Evan's initial request. He'd stapled Dave Hawthorne's card to the report. If the reporter made a nuisance of himself, Evan might just follow through on his threat to ferret out his buddy at the IRS.

The second report gave the status of the Department of Justice's efforts to locate Jonah Dawes, the man who'd bilked hundreds of Missy Marie's fans of their savings.

The third report was the one that clenched Evan's muscles.

Dammit, why didn't she answer her phone?

Yanking at the knot in his tie, he spun around to stare through the windows behind his desk. One of the few benefits of rising to the top of the assistant D.A. ranks was a corner office. Not that the panoramic view of San Diego's harbor actually compensated for the killer caseload and seven-day workweeks that came with the seniority. If anything, the sparkling bay and colorful sailboats scudding across the waves only emphasized how infrequently Evan got to enjoy either.

Normally he didn't mind his grinding schedule. The challenges of his job usually brought their own rewards. Take this afternoon, for example. They'd spent months building the government's case against Hector Mendoza, and the Grand Jury had needed less than two hours to return an indictment. The bastard now faced ten counts of violating U.S. immigration laws, thirty-two counts of conspiring to violate those laws, eighteen counts of involuntary manslaughter and six counts of drug trafficking.

To Evan's intense satisfaction, the judge had bound the scuzz over for trial and set bail at a cool two million. It was little enough considering the eighteen men, women and children who'd suffocated to death during a botched attempt to smuggle them across the border in one of Mendoza's petroleum transport rigs. As icing on the cake, a sweating Joey Smallwood had fingered dozens of cogs in Mendoza's extensive narcotics smuggling and distribution network. Search and arrest warrants were being served all up and down the coast.

Now the real work would begin in Mendoza's case. A small army of prosecuting and defense attorneys would slug it out during discovery, file motions and counter motions, and generally try to rip out each others' throat during the actual trial. And this was only one of the two dozen or so cases Evan had working.

Blowing out a long breath, he jingled the change in his pants pockets. He should go out and join the impromptu celebration Carrie had organized to celebrate the indictment. Champagne corks and pizza carton lids had started popping the moment the D.A. wound up his press conference. As lead attorney on the case, Evan intended to claim at least two or three slices of pepperoni.

He'd try one more call first, this one to Charlie.

He was reaching for the phone when Carrie strolled in carrying two plastic cups. The thrill of victory still tinted her cheeks and sparkled in her green eyes.

"I brought you some bubbly."

"Thanks. I'll be out to join the fun in a minute."

Ignoring the unsubtle hint, Carrie bumped the door shut an agile hip and found a perch on the corner of Evan's desk. With a slither of nylon, she crossed her legs. Her slim navy skirt rode up on her thighs. A spiked heel swung from one stockinged toe.

"I thought we might conduct our own private celebration," she purred. "Very private."

Evan replaced the receiver and mentally braced himself for another round in the battle of wills that had broken out during the drive back from Paradise.

"We talked about this, Carrie."

"I've decided that's the problem," she told him with a smile. "Instead of talking, we should do what we did so well together."

"Why don't we just drink to what we do *best* together?"

Reaching for one of the plastic cups, Evan tipped her a salute.

"Nice summation this afternoon, Counselor."

Perfectly outlined red lips pouted, but she raised her glass to his. "Thanks."

She took a slow sip, eyeing him over the rim. A flinty edge of anger had replaced the pout by the time the cup lowered.

"You're not going to give our relationship another chance, are you?"

He refrained from pointing out that one brief encounter did not a relationship make.

"It wouldn't work for either one of us, Carrie."

"Funny, you didn't seem so sure of that until your little side trip through the desert." An oval crimson nail tapped plastic. "Does your change of heart have anything to do with that blonde who...?"

A sharp rap on the door interrupted her interrogation. She flushed with annoyance when Evan's assistant stuck her head inside.

"Sorry to interrupt. The mayor's on the boss's private line. He needs you in his office to answer a few questions."

"Okay." Setting his cup on the desk, Evan nodded to Carrie. "I'll be right back, and we'll finish this conversation."

Tight with anger, Carrie tossed back her champagne and reached for Evan's. The set of his jaw told her their conversation was already finished. *They* were finished, not that they'd ever really begun. All that remained was the wake.

It stung her pride that he'd been the one to put the skids on what could have been a helluva ride for both of them. She'd known all along she was pushing him too hard. Known, too, he wasn't the kind of man who could be pushed. That in itself had represented a challenge, and Carrie thrived on challenges.

She'd pulled every string in the book to wrangle this special detail. Including, she recalled with a grimace, making nicey-nice with a particularly repellent DOJ regional director. The director was only a means to an end. She'd had her sights set on Evan from the first time she'd met him at a conference. Getting to work with him on a high-profile case was a double bonus.

Evan didn't know it, but he'd been her prime target from the day she'd landed at the San Diego airport. She'd wanted to add the lean, handsome assistant D.A. to her trophy rack almost as much as she wanted to add an indictment in the Mendoza case to her impressive list of credits.

She'd bagged one of her quarries, but the fact that the other had sidestepped her snare destroyed much of her pleasure in the victory.

She slid off the desk, forgetting about the cup in her hand until it sloshed champagne onto a stack of files. Cursing, Carrie tore a couple of sheets off a notepad to blot the spill. She was dabbing at the champagne when the handwritten label on the top folder caught her attention.

"Lissa. Well, well, well."

Without a qualm, she flipped the folder open and skimmed its contents.

The call to the mayor dragged on for a good half hour. Worried about the fact that he'd unknowingly hired one of Mendoza's customers as a nanny for his children, the politician tried to pin Evan down as to whether he'd be called to testify during the trial.

"We don't start discovery for another two weeks," Evan replied to the disembodied voice coming through the speakerphone. "I want to see who the defense intends to call before I decide who I'll put on the stand."

"You've got all the ammunition you need with Smallwood," the mayor protested.

"His testimony helped bring in the indictment, but I'm going to drive home every nail I can to convict that bastard."

"Don't screw with me, Henderson. You know damn well I plan to announce my candidacy for a second term during the President's visit next month."

The mayor left unsaid that U.S. district attorneys were appointed by the President, but the message came through loud and clear. If Evan harbored any ambition to move into his boss's office when he retired next year, he'd better tread carefully. Very carefully.

Evan didn't particularly care for either the message or its sender.

"I'll let you know," he said coolly.

The sound of a phone crashing down reverberated through the speaker. R. Harrison Burke laced his fingers across his shirtfront, propped an Italian loafer on a desk drawer and angled back his chair.

"You're not going to score many points that way, Ev."

"I'll worry about scoring points after we send Mendoza down."

"Well, if anyone's going to do it, you will. Tell me who you want on your trial team."

"Teresa Lopez, for sure. And Lowenstein. If we extend Carrie Northcutt's detail through the trial date, that should give me enough brainpower."

Burke lifted a shaggy brow. "You want Northcutt's detail extended? I got the feeling things had cooled off between you two."

Whatever his personal feelings for Carrie, Evan would never deny her skill or her professionalism. She'd jump at the chance to follow through with the case she'd already put so many weeks of intense work into.

"She's one of the sharpest minds in DOJ, Harry. If we can keep her, let's do it."

"Good enough." The Italian loafers hit the floor with a thump. "We'd better get back to the party before the pizza's gone, then blow this place. You need to lift your face to the sun while you can. It's probably the last time you'll see daylight until after Mendoza's trial."

Evan shagged a hand through his hair, knowing Harry had that right. Knowing, too, he needed to talk to Lissa before the trial engulfed him.

"Listen, Harry, I need to go out of town for a couple of days."

"Again? You just got back."

"Yeah, I know."

"What's the problem?"

"No problem. Just some personal business I need to take care of."

Burke didn't like it, but he was all too aware of the fact that Evan forfeited twice as many weeks of unused vacation time each year than anyone else in the district. The director of personnel in D.C. chastised the D.A. regularly for failing to ensure his people took the time they were entitled to.

"All right, but leave me a number," he grumbled. "If the mayor calls again, I'll have him transferred to you at wherever it is you're heading. Where are you going, anyway?"

"Paradise," Evan replied with a grin. "I'm on my way to Paradise."

"I'll find no greater love
This side of Hea-'vn.
I'll seek no greater joy,
This side of Par-a-dise."

Grimacing, Lissa ended the last bar two beats short of a full measure. The B-flat wasn't enough of a stretch, didn't deliver the emotion she wanted. Grabbing her stubby pencil, she erased the scribbled notes and tried another variation.

There. A quarter note, two eighths slurred together, and a soaring, joyful E half note tied over to a whole in the final bar.

Her fingers curved over the keyboard, she found the d.s. that marked the beginning of the refrain and cleared her throat. It felt more than a little raw from the hours she'd been hammering away at the refrain, but she hit the keys with single-minded determination.

For the first seventeen bars, she blended chords, melody and lyrics perfectly. On the last syllable, her voice cracked and she missed the E completely.

"Well, horsefeathers!"

Fisting her hands, she thumped the keys in frustration. The discordant jangle did little to soothe her frazzled nerves.

She'd been trying to finish this blasted song for almost a week now. Henderson's presence in Paradise had proved too distracting for Lissa to work on it while he was here. To her profound irritation, his absence was proving even more unsettling.

Why couldn't she put the man out of her head? Why in thunder did that kiss at the dam keep snaking back into her thoughts? Henderson had just been killing time. The green-eyed cat who'd sharpened her claws on Lissa had made that perfectly clear. He'd been playing with her, and like a fool, she'd joined right in his games. Disgust rolled through her every time she remembered the way she'd practically melted in his arms.

One of these days, she'd learn to…

A barrage of furious barking erupted under the trailer.

Lissa jumped half out of her skin. Her heart thudding against her ribs, she leaned over the keyboard to peer through the blinds. A single, powerful beam stabbed the night.

A motorcycle headlight!

Disbelief raced along her nerves, tightened her chest. She jerked upright, her fists jarring another squawk from the keys. For a moment, she considered letting Henderson duke it out with Wolf. Reluctantly she realized she couldn't allow the dog to take a chunk out of his rear…as much as she'd like to!

The Harley roared its way up the slope. Wolf's barking slid into toe-curling snarls.

Panicked now that she'd waited too long and the dog would launch an airborne attack on his victim, Lissa shoved away from the table. Her chair crashed to the floor behind her as she jumped for the door.

"Wolf! Down…!"

The dog froze in a half crouch. What looked like a two-inch thick T-bone dangled from his jaws.

"Let him have it," a deep voice drawled. "I hauled the thing all the way from San Diego packed in dry ice, figuring I'd have to bribe my way past him."

Lissa's incredulous gaze swung to Evan. He sat

astride his bike, a boot planted on either side. Dragging off his helmet, he hooked it on a handlebar.

"Hello, Lissa."

"What are you doing here?" She pitched the question over Wolf's whine. "I thought you and your friend had a big case to work."

"We did. The Grand Jury returned the indictments we asked for this afternoon."

"Congratula..." Another long, piteous whine drowned out her sarcastic response. "Oh, all right. Scarf it down. Go on, take it."

That was all the encouragement Wolf needed. With a single leap, he and the slab of T-bone disappeared under the trailer.

"Back to my original question." She folded her arms across her chest and treated him to a frosty stare. "What are you doing here?"

He heeled down the kickstand and swung off the bike. "Before I answer that, suppose you tell me why you haven't answered your phone for the past few days."

"I've been working."

It was a pitiful excuse, but Lissa wasn't ready to admit that she'd been so angry with herself for falling for his line, she'd set her jaw every time the phone rang and ignored it. Or tried to.

Obviously not any happier with her excuse than she was, he strode to the front steps. One boot rang on metal before he realized she wasn't going to move.

"I told you I'd call."

"There were a couple of things you *didn't* tell me, Henderson."

Light spilled over her shoulder and painted his face in sharp angles. "Such as?"

"Such as the fact that you're involved with Ms. Legal Beagle."

"I *was* involved with Carrie," he admitted. "I'm not now."

"Oh?" Sarcasm dripped like the battery acid that rusted the dirt under her pickup. "Is she— what's her name…Carrie?—aware of that?"

"Yes."

"Just out of curiosity, when did this big breakup occur? Before or after we took a detour to the Painted Rocks Dam?"

"Before, although I guess I didn't cut the tie as cleanly as I should have." He planted a boot on the next step. It brought him several inches closer to her. Several inches too close. "The last thread snapped when you laid that Saturday Afternoon Special on me."

Angry heat rushed into her cheeks. "If you want to climb back on your bike with all your limbs intact, you won't mention *any* kind of a special to me again."

He laughed at her. The smooth-talking, oversexed, muscle-bound jerk actually laughed at her! Right before he took the top step.

Lissa gave serious thought to planting both hands on his chest and shoving. Hard. She wouldn't mind seeing his butt hit the dirt, followed by his grin. Only the realization that she probably couldn't budge him kept her arms crossed and her dignity intact.

Still one step down, Evan decided he'd found the perfect positioning. They were shoulder-to-shoulder, eye to smoldering eye. Her nose couldn't be more than three inches from his. Her mouth...

His stomach clenched. The clamp he'd kept on his fantasies during the long ride from San Diego snapped. Greedy desire shot straight to his groin as he remembered the feel of her warm, wet mouth under his.

He dragged his gaze from her lips, only to grind his teeth at the way her hair feathered her shoulders. If she'd been wearing something besides those cutoffs and a spaghetti-strap tank top, he might not have gotten so hard so fast. But she was, and he did.

He knew darn well she'd put a good-size dent in both his ego and his manhood if he leaned forward and kissed her smooth, creamy shoulder the way he ached to. That would come, he promised. After he'd regained her trust...and after she'd recovered from the bomb he was about to drop on her.

"Let me come in, Lissa. We need to talk."

"We don't *need* to do anything, Henderson."

She had that one hundred percent wrong, but he didn't argue.

"It's Evan," he reminded her with a calm that tightened her jaw. "Let me come in. I have some information you'll want to hear."

The stubbornness he suspected was bred into her along with her incredible talent held her rooted for another few moments. Finally, grudgingly, she dropped her arms and retreated a few paces.

Only a few. She didn't invite him to sit down. Didn't offer him a cool drink.

"Well?"

"I told you I'd run some queries. I was curious to see if the databases we have access to would turn up any shady characters in or around La-Grange."

"Besides me, you mean?"

He didn't bother to reply to that. "Do you remember the attendant at the convenience store? The one who helped you pump gas last week?"

"Vaguely." Her brows slanted. "Why?"

"The tag on his uniform gave his name as Arlen," Evan said slowly. "I ran that against the tattoo on his left arm and came up with a hit. A man matching his description has been arrested a half-dozen times in almost as many states for drunk and disorderly conduct. His last arrest occurred two and a half years ago."

"And I'm interested in this because…?"

Evan dragged in a deep breath. There was no way to soften the blow. "Arlen's his middle name, Lissa. One of two, as a matter of fact. His full name is Robert Stockton Arlen James."

Shock flooded her eyes. She stumbled back, shaking her head in a wild arc. "I don't believe it!"

"I double-checked with the Oklahoma Bureau of Vital Statistics. The birth dates, blood type and names all match. He's your father."

Chapter 10

A helpless sympathy grabbed at Evan as he watched emotions rain down on Lissa like hail. Shock, disbelief, denial all bombarded her. For a moment, only a moment, he glimpsed a pain so raw it sliced the breath right out of his lungs.

Coming from a large, rambunctious family, where everyone shared everyone else's joys and sorrows, he couldn't begin to imagine the hurt of knowing your only blood relative was a stranger living just ten miles away. A stranger who either didn't recognize or didn't want to acknowledge you. Evan ached to comfort her, to lessen her shock and hurt. But Lissa, being Lissa, rejected the pain just as she tried to reject him.

"I…" Her throat working, she struggled to find her footing after the body blow he'd just dealt her. "I appreciate that you rode all the way back to Paradise to tell me about this."

That was only one of several reasons he'd come back, but she didn't need to hear the rest of them now.

"If you don't mind, I need to—" lifting a shaky hand, she swiped back her bangs "—think."

No way Evan was leaving her alone to deal with this. Not until her eyes lost their bruised look, anyway.

"Think sitting down," he suggested as a tremor shook her and she reached unsteadily for the back of a kitchen chair.

"No, I…"

"Sit down."

He enforced the order with a gentle tug on her arm that deposited her in the chair.

A tiny spark of annoyance cut through Lissa's suffocating emotions, but she couldn't deal with Henderson right now. She could hardly deal with the fragmented images that spun through her mind like an out-of-control Ferris wheel. Over and over she saw the gravel road outside the Baptist Children's Home, still wet from the spring rain that had fallen the morning her father drove off. The ragged Pooh Bear she'd clutched in her arms. The McNabbs' faces when they tried to explain why Lissa had been left with them.

Juxtapositioned over these searing memories was the hazy face of the hollow-cheeked attendant who'd pumped gas into her pickup a week ago.

She was only vaguely aware of Evan poking around the trailer's tiny kitchen. Hardly registered the bump of his knee against hers as he plunked a glass of iced tea down in front of her. He took the other chair, not crowding her, not pressing her for the chaotic thoughts that slowly sorted themselves out in her confused brain...until finally she was left with only one.

It didn't matter. Whether or not the man at the convenience store was her father made no difference at this point in her life. Robert James had abandoned her as a child, when she'd needed him most. As a result, she'd made her own way in the world. A rocky way for the past few years, but her own way nevertheless. She'd known love and joy with the McNabbs, and found happiness in her music. That was all she needed. All she wanted.

Or all she *had* wanted until a stupid, silly kiss beside a dam had started her thinking about what she was missing.

Resentment fluttered in her chest. Blast Evan Henderson! Since he'd barged into her life, he'd taken her on a wild, roller-coaster ride from wary distrust to shaken wonder to fury. She'd almost convinced herself she was well rid of him when he roared up the hill with this piece of shattering news and started the cycle all over again.

He caught the look she flashed him and interpreted it as a signal she was ready to break the charged silence.

"Do you remember your father?"

Lissa didn't want to answer, but she supposed she owed him something for coming all this way to deliver the news personally.

"All I remember is watching him drive away."

"Did you ever discover why he left?"

"Reverend McNabb told me he sorrowed so much over my mother's death that he couldn't give me the joy and happiness a child needs." Her fingers curled around the dew-streaked glass. "Or the love, apparently."

She lifted the tea, needing something to ease a throat suddenly gone tight and dry. Behind a thick screen of sun-tipped brown lashes, Evan's blue eyes followed her every movement.

"We have to assume he knows who you are," he said when she'd gulped down a long, soothing swallow. "The odds that he'd turn up practically on your doorstep by chance must hover right around a couple of billion to one. My bet is he tracked you to Paradise."

"By opening the mail that went to the McNabbs."

"It makes sense. He of all people would know about your connection to them."

The tea puddled in Lissa's stomach. Quite a man, her father. He dumped his only child in the road and drove off without a backward glance, spent the next twenty or so years in a drunken haze and apparently didn't blink at rifling through other people's mail.

"I'm surprised he's waited so long since spotting me in LaGrange to try to hit me up for money."

She winced inwardly at the bitterness coating her comment, but the naive girl who once sang for the sheer joy of it had learned her lesson all too well.

"You think that's why he's tracked you down?"

"Why else?"

"I guess we won't know until we talk to him."

"*We're* not going to talk to him," Lissa shot back. "Either separately or collectively. This isn't any of your business, Evan."

"Right," he drawled. "That's what I kept telling myself during the three-hour ride back to Paradise."

She had the grace to flush. "I told you, I appreciate that you made the long trip to tell me about my father. Now…"

"Now I can just climb back on my bike and head home again, is that it?"

Her chin came up. "Yes."

"Not this time, Lissa."

"Excuse me?"

"I left the last time with things unsettled between us. I'm not going to make that mistake again.''

Coming on top of the emotional bomb he'd just detonated, his calm assumption that there was anything between them to settle fired her fuse all over again.

"Back up a minute, fella! There is no 'us.'"

"Don't you think that verdict is a bit premature? I haven't presented all my arguments in the case yet."

"I don't believe you!" Lissa exploded out of her chair. "You show up out of the blue and inform me that the father I haven't seen or heard from in more than twenty years now lives just ten miles away. Then, before I can take a breath, you start playing lawyer games with me. Is this what they teach you in law school? Always keep your witnesses off balance? Is that the only way you can get past their defenses?"

"I figured out the day I met you, it's the only way I can get past yours." Unabashed and completely unrepentant, he came to his feet and smiled down at her. "You're as prickly as a cholla, sweetheart, and twice as sharp."

The smile infuriated Lissa almost as much as the tenderness behind it. She couldn't handle either right now. Maybe not ever.

He must have seen that her frazzled nerves were about to shred apart. "Don't look so panicked," he said gently. "We'll sort everything out."

Feeling absurdly cornered by his gentleness, Lissa scrubbed the heel of her hand across her forehead. She needed to think, needed to work through her confusion and the stabbing hurt that refused to go away at the thought of her father. Most of all, she needed Evan out of her trailer before she did something absolutely insane. Like yield to the idiotic urge to take him up on that "we." Or plant herself against his solid chest and bawl her eyes out.

"I think you'd better go."

"You sure? I'm a good listener. We can talk. Or not talk, if that's what you want."

She shook her head, fighting the lump that insisted on forming in her throat. Evan grinning down at her with that maddening glint in his eyes she could resist...barely! Evan quiet and gentle and offering to share her burdens she couldn't handle. She wouldn't...couldn't...trust another man with her fears and feelings. Wrapping her arms around her waist, she waited for him to leave.

Evan reined in the need that gnawed at his gut. With everything in him, he ached to take Lissa in his arms. He could see the hairline cracks in her brittle shell, see the hurt she tried so hard to disguise. She was going to hold it all in, every emotion, every pain, the way she had for the past three years. And there wasn't a damned thing Evan could do about it until she lowered her barriers enough to let him inside.

"I called ahead to ask Josephine to put me up," he told her. "You can reach me at her place if you need me tonight. Otherwise, I'll see you in the morning."

She didn't argue, which should have raised Evan's suspicions right then and there. But it wasn't until he'd forced himself to the door and hit the first step that his instincts grabbed hold. He turned back, his boot scraping on the metal step, and felt his lungs shut down.

Lissa was slumped against the trailer's frowzy pecan paneling. Eyes closed, palms braced against the wall, she waged a silent battle to keep from admitting her defenses had been breached. The single, silvery tear that traced a path down her cheek told Evan she'd lost the battle.

Brutal need slammed into him. He could no more stop to analyze its intensity than he could force his lungs to function. His chest aching, he crossed the shag carpet in two strides and gathered her in his arms.

"It's okay, Lissa. It's okay. We'll work out whatever needs working."

She resisted, or tried to. Evan wasn't letting her push him away again. He stroked her hair, felt her tremble as the barriers crumpled, one after the other. Warm dampness seeped through his shirt and burned his into skin. The ache that had wrapped around his heart squeezed tight.

"Shh, sweetheart. Don't cry. We can…"

"I'm *not* crying," she wailed against his shirt-front. "I never cry."

Evan was no stranger to women's tears. Men's, either, for that matter. He'd cracked too many witnesses on the stand and watched in satisfaction as juries pronounced too many sentences to suffer any remorse for having caused a grown man or woman to weep.

The ridiculous helplessness he felt at this moment was new to him, however. His hand maintained its steady stroke. His arm kept its hold around Lissa's waist. Yet every sob, every desperate attempt to choke back her tears, tore at his soul.

He was floundering in a totally unfamiliar sea of incompetence when a low, dangerous growl lifted the hairs on the back of his neck. He shot a look over one shoulder, bracing for what he'd find. Wolf crouched half in, half out of the open trailer door, his eyes slitted and his gums quivering above yellowed fangs. Whatever temporary truce Evan might have won with that T-bone had evaporated. The dog's shaggy ruff stood straight up, his ears pointed straight back.

Evan formed the unmistakable impression he'd forfeit a chunk of his backside if he didn't loosen his hold on Lissa in the next two and a half seconds. His muscles tightened in anticipation, particularly those within lunging distance of the half-wild creature. Yet he was damned if he could let go of the woman whose rasping sobs were only now starting to lessen.

"Easy, boy. I'm not hurting her."

Either the quiet warning in his voice or Wolf's answering snarl pierced Lissa's misery. She lifted her head and peered around Evan's shoulder.

"It's okay." She got out the words on a watery sniffle, unconsciously echoing Evan's assurances of a moment ago. "It's okay, Wolf."

The issue remained in doubt for another few seconds, and wasn't decided until Lissa pushed out of Evan's arms and regained command of her voice.

"It's okay, boy. Go outside. Go on outside."

With a final look at Evan that promised violent retribution if he crossed the line again, the dog backed down the steps.

His potential victim unclenched his buttocks and turned back to Lissa. She was struggling valiantly to recover from her brief lapse into what he guessed she'd construe as weakness.

Sure enough, she swiped the back of a hand across a nose red from embarrassment as much as from her crying jag. "I'm sorry. I don't know why…I've never…" She took another determined swipe. "I'm not usually such a ninny."

"Neither am I," Evan admitted. "I figured my news would hit you hard. I should have given you more time to absorb the shock before I laid the next one on you."

"The next one being the fact that you want to take up where we left off at the dam?"

"That's the one." Despite himself, he had to smile as he reached out to thumb teary residue from her cheek. "It doesn't take you long to recover, does it?"

A sigh slipped through her lips. "Seems like it's taking longer and longer these days."

She nibbled on her lower lip for a moment, studying him through spiked lashes. Evan wasn't sure what was coming next, and realized he was holding his breath.

"Did you mean what you said earlier?"

He searched his memory. "About that kiss at the dam snapping the last thread? It's true, Lissa. There really wasn't anything between Carrie and me when I drove my Harley into a ditch."

"I believe you," she conceded after a long moment. "But that's not what I was asking."

"What then?"

She worried her lower lip again, looked away, brought her tear-washed eyes back to his.

"Did you mean it when you said we could just talk?"

"Absolutely," he lied.

"Or..." She drew in a shuddering breath, met his gaze with a hesitancy that kicked him right in his libidinous middle. "Not talk?"

"That depends on what *you* mean by not talking," he replied cautiously, ordering his stomach not to tighten and his glands not to produce a sudden sweat. After feeling her body trembling against his, he'd cut off his right arm before he pushed her too hard, too fast, again.

Lissa shuddered again. The struggle on her face hurt to watch.

"Hold me, Evan. Please. Just hold me. It's been so long since I... Since anyone..."

He whirled and stomped away while she was still stammering out her request. His palm cracked against the door and slammed it into place. For good measure, he twisted the old-fashioned lock before he strode back to her, smiling at her startled expression.

"Just making sure I don't lose a piece of my tail to your shaggy protector," he said as he scooped her into his arms.

He sank into the trailer's only armchair, taking her with him. Legs out, body angled, he settled her weight against his own. She held herself stiff and awkward for a few moments, as if already regretting her impulsive request, then slowly, so slowly, relaxed.

Evan only wished he could do the same. He willed his muscles not to respond to the feel of her hips nestling into his, but there wasn't much he could do about his senses. With every breath, he drew in her sun-washed scent. With every knock of his heart, he felt an answering beat through the soft breast pressed against his chest. He could taste desire hot and metallic on his tongue, hear his pulse hammering in his ears. But the hand that tunneled under her hair to massage her knotted neck muscles was slow and sure and gentle.

He had no idea how many minutes or hours passed before she sighed and curled her head into the hollow between his shoulder and neck. No idea how long he held her, getting hotter by degrees with each moist breath that washed against his skin. His watch was buried under her hair, and his mind had shut down to everything but the absolute, iron-willed determination not to acknowledge the growing ache in his groin.

That ache didn't compare to the agony that exploded when she shifted a little in his lap. His back teeth ground together. Despite his best efforts, he couldn't hold back a little grunt. At the sound, she tipped her head back, adding another electric jolt.

"Am I too heavy?"

He unlocked his jaw to give her what he hoped was a smile. "No."

"Are you sure?"

Sweat pooled at the base of his spine. "Yes. I just need to shift my legs a little."

Remorse chased across her face as he flexed his thigh muscles to lift her an inch or two.

"I didn't think. I bet your legs have gone to sleep."

He wished! The needles shooting through his

lower body had nothing to do with sleep. Not the kind she referred to, anyway.

"I'll get off." She wiggled upright. "I didn't mean to…"

"Don't move!"

He tried to soften the terse order with one of his cocky grins, but suspected it came up considerably short of his usual standards.

"You're okay right there, Lissa."

He wished to hell he could say the same for himself. But if she moved another inch, he'd be in serious trouble here. Very serious trouble.

Evan couldn't believe he was so close to losing control. He hadn't felt this kind of cramping ache since he'd developed a consuming passion for Mary Alice Janecke in the fifth grade. As he recalled, his smirking older brother had found him trying to hide the embarrassing results of that passion from their mother's eagle eye. Jake had taken him into town the very next day to buy his first package of condoms.

Evan had carried that foil pack in his wallet for years. Fortunately, by the time he got around to needing it, he'd figured out that dry, cracked rubber wouldn't do the trick. Now he replaced his supplies regularly. Just the thought of the emergency stash tucked into the wallet in his back pocket knotted his gut.

The sudden comprehension in Lissa's eyes knotted it even more. She didn't breathe, didn't move, thank God, except to suck in a gulp of air.

"Evan, I'm not sure..."

"I know."

"I mean, I'm not ready...."

"I know." His grin came a little easier this time. "I won't make the same claim myself, but that doesn't mean I can't hold you. Just hold you," he added as a protest formed in her eyes.

She trembled, like a bird gathering its strength to take wing.

"You can trust me, Lissa," Evan said softly. "Put your head on my shoulder."

Chapter 11

A series of sharp raps against the trailer door dragged Lissa from a deep, dreamless sleep. She mumbled a protest, squeezing her eyes tight as she burrowed her face into the pillow.

The rapper hit the door again, louder and irritatingly insistent. She had just opened her mouth to tell whoever was making the racket to *go away* when her pillow moved under her cheek.

Her head jerked up. Her lids popped open. Two sleepy blue eyes smiled into hers.

"'Mornin', sweetheart."

Morning?

She fired a disbelieving glance at the sunlight streaming through the blinds. A groan started deep in her belly. It was halfway to her throat when another series of whacks assaulted her ears.

"It's me," a voice called impatiently. "Josephine. Open the door, you two. This dish is heavy."

It took some doing, but Lissa resisted the urge to bury her face in Evan's wrinkled denim shirt once more. She'd never run from a mess of her own making in her life. She wasn't about to start now.

That firm resolution didn't keep her face from flaming as she scooted off Evan's lap. Or heating a dozen more degrees when she opened the door and Josephine's rhinestone-ringed eyes zipped right past her to the man sprawled in the easy chair, one arm raised to rub his stiff neck. Glee sparkled in the gaze Josephine turned on Lissa.

"I took this cornflakes and pork chop hash out of the freezer when Evan called last night to say he was on his way back to Paradise. It's just as good for breakfast as it is for dinner."

Brushing by Lissa, the Widow Jenks marched into the trailer on zebra-striped mules topped with bright red powder puffs and deposited her burden on the kitchen table. Hands mittened by hot pads went to her ample hips, covered by tight leggings patterned in the same, eye-opening white-and-black stripes as her mules.

"You should've let me know you wouldn't be needing my spare room after all, young man."

Evan rose to his feet, nodding apologetically. "Yes, ma'am, I should have."

"I worried about you until Charlie stopped by to tell me he saw your bike parked outside Lissa's trailer last night."

Tapping five, red-painted toes, she looked him over from his rumpled hair to the wrinkled shirt-tails hanging out of his jeans.

"Well, go scrape those cactus branches off your face. This hash turns soggy when it cools."

"Yes, ma'am," he said again, hiding a smile behind the hand he rasped across his bristling chin. "I'll get my shaving gear from my bike."

Lissa stood as still as a rock until he returned from his brief foray outside. She didn't say a word when he squeezed past her. Neither did he. But the lazy kiss he dropped on her nose before he headed down the narrow hallway to her bird's-nest-size bathroom trumpeted its own message. Lissa's cheeks scorched with heat as Josephine hooted and clapped her oven mitts together in pure delight.

"Way to go, girl! I was starting to think you'd never leave Paradise. Now I'll get to watch you cruise out of town on the back of a Harley."

"I'm not cruising anywhere, and certainly not on the back of a Harley." Raking a hand through her bangs, Lissa attempted a muddled explanation. "This isn't what it looks like."

That earned her another hoot.

"Honestly. We just sort of…fell asleep."

"I'd fall asleep in that man's lap, too, if he'd sit still long enough for me to climb into it!"

She gave up, submitting helplessly to the pat on the cheek Josephine bestowed on her in parting.

"Paradise is a nice little bit of heaven for dried-up old coots like Charlie and me. You need more. You *deserve* more. Reach out and grab the gold ring, sweetie."

Evan pushed the same general advice at her when he emerged from the bathroom a few moments later.

Lissa tried, she really tried, not to notice the fleck of shaving foam he'd missed at the base of his throat. The tiny blob would've been a lot easier to ignore if he'd gotten around to buttoning his shirt all the way up before he strolled into the living area. His skin gleamed like bronze through the wrinkled denim.

"Did Josephine leave?"

"Yes."

Idly he finished the last of the buttons and shoved his shirttails into his jeans. "Have you ever tried her cornflakes hash?" he asked, tipping the cover on the dish to eye the oval-shaped loaf cautiously.

"No, but I can fix you some eggs and toast if you'd rather have something more traditional before you head back to San Diego this morning."

He tipped her a smile in response to her obvious

exploratory probe. "I'm not heading back to San Diego this morning. I'm going into LaGrange with you to scope out your father."

Ignoring her sudden stiffening, he poked around in her cupboards for the plates.

"Better wash up quick," he advised. "This stuff doesn't smell half-bad."

It smelled like onions, pork chops and cheesy cornflakes. Crazy as it sounded, Lissa's taste buds had already sat up and taken notice. Her appetite had been off all week...because of the bone-melting heat, she'd determined, *not* Henderson's departure from Paradise with his cat-eyed friend.

"About LaGrange. I don't want to..."

"Go wash up. We'll talk about it while we eat."

He accompanied this brisk order with another kiss, this one on lips closed tight over teeth she hadn't yet brushed. Lissa decided to wait until she finished in the bathroom to tell him she didn't particularly appreciate his habit of issuing orders like a drill sergeant.

After a quick face-and-teeth scrub, she dragged a comb through her hair, exchanged her tank top for a sleeveless, V-necked T-shirt in a startling hot pink and returned to the kitchen.

"I don't want to go into LaGrange this morning," she announced, prepared to do battle if necessary. She needed time to sort out her feelings about the convenience store clerk who just happened to share her last name. A lot of time.

"Okay. I made coffee."

Thoroughly suspicious at his easy capitulation, she took the mug he passed her and joined him at the table. The hash loaf, she noted, was now missing a good-size chunk at one end.

"I was only going to sneak a taste," he admitted with a sheepish grin. "One sneak led to another. Josephine has a way with cornflakes." He spooned generous helpings onto two plates. "Why the heck is she wasting her culinary talent and all those rhinestones in Paradise?"

"She's in love with Charlie."

Evan's eyes widened. The forkful of hash halfway to his mouth stopped in midair.

A smile played at Lissa's lips. She guessed he was trying to process an image of squat, barrel-chested Charlie and the Widow Jenks in a clinch. The mechanic would stand just about eye-level with Josephine's magnificent cleavage.

"Is this, uh, a recent development?"

"I think it happened in 1956." A full-fledged smile slipped out of Lissa. "Josephine told me he bent over to check the water in the radiator of her brand-new '56 Ford Fairlane. She took one look at his buns and decided right then and there to stay in Paradise instead of driving on to California, as she'd intended."

Josephine certainly hadn't hesitated to reach out and grab for the gold, she thought, pushing the hash around on her plate. She'd lost her husband

of one week, then found a love that had endured
for four decades.

Still ruminating over Josephine's parting words
of advice, Lissa glanced up to surprise a wicked
glint in Evan's eyes.

"Sometimes one glimpse of really world-class
buns is all it takes," he told her solemnly. "The
first time you climbed out of your pickup and bent
over to pick up my wallet, I thought I'd died and
gone to…paradise."

Heat crawled up Lissa's neck. She shoveled in
a bite of hash and clamped her lips around her fork
to keep from having to answer.

After that, they polished off their breakfast in
relative silence. Evan finished his long before
Lissa, then contented himself with a second cup of
coffee and watching her pick her way through the
hash. With each moment his gaze rested on her,
she found it harder and harder to swallow. Her
nerves were tap-dancing against her spine when he
broke into her chaotic thoughts.

"So what do you want to do this morning if
we're not going into LaGrange?"

There it was again. That "we."

"I don't know what you're going to do, but I
have to finish…"

"That won't work, Lissa. You can't shut me out
again. Not after spending last night in my arms."

"Last night was…" She flapped a hand. "A
fluke. A temporary weakness."

"You think so?"

"I know so."

She didn't convince herself any more than her listener. Evan studied her face for a long moment, then pushed away from the table and reached down a hand.

"Let's put it to the test."

Lissa stared at his broad palm and blunt-tipped fingers with the same startled fascination as a rabbit coming nose-to-nose with a sidewinder. Surely to goodness he wasn't proposing another session in the armchair? Or... She gulped. A trip down the hall to the bedroom?

Without warning, her womb contracted. So hard and fast her breath caught. The ripple effect spread like liquid fire through her lower belly. She gulped again and jerked her gaze up to his face.

The wicked glint was back in his eyes, as though he'd read her mind...or more correctly, the silent message her body was screaming at her. Rationally she refused to acknowledge the tight sensations at the juncture of her thighs. Irrationally every atom of her femininity ached to take his hand and lead him to her bed.

"Come with me, Lissa."

She wet her lips. "Where?"

"You can trust me, sweetheart. Just like you did last night."

Could she trust herself?

"Take my hand."

It was a test. She knew it. He knew it. Could she reach out, go for the gold? Now that she'd recovered from the awful emptiness learning about her father had caused last night, did she have the courage to walk into Evan's arms again?

She pulled in a breath. Forced her heart to pump some blood to her frantic brain. Put her hand in his.

He led her from the table toward the hall...but not down the narrow corridor. Instead he opened the front door and flooded the trailer with dazzling sunlight. Still holding her hand, he guided her down the steps. Lissa blinked as morning heat engulfed her, not as intense as it would be in an hour or so, but dry and searing nonetheless.

Wolf scrambled out from under the trailer and lifted his gums in a warning quiver. He couldn't quite figure out what was going on. Lissa couldn't, either.

"Here, put this on."

"What in the world...?"

"We'll take a long cruise." He plunked the electric-blue fiberglass helmet on her head and fiddled with the strap. "Blow away the cobwebs from last night and start fresh."

She couldn't tell him that she'd already started. That all it took was the feel of his knuckles brushing the underside of her chin to raise instant goose bumps. She remembered all too well the last time his hand had skimmed that particular patch of skin.

At the dam. Just before he'd collected that Saturday Afternoon Special.

She was still trying to banish the memory when he slipped on his sunglasses and swung a leg over the saddle. Hauling the Harley upright, he popped its kickstand with his left heel. A flick of the key and a twist of the throttle produced a muscled growl that swiftly morphed into an unmannered roar. Reaching behind him, Evan patted the seat.

"Climb aboard and I'll show you what this Hawg can do."

"I've seen what it can do," Lissa retorted, hanging back. "I haven't forgotten what your back looked like when I picked you up."

"Will it help if I tell you that was my first and only dive into a ditch in twenty-plus years of biking?"

"Well..."

His white teeth flashed against tanned skin. "Tell you what. If you collect any scrapes or bruises on this ride, I'll kiss 'em and make 'em well...wherever they are."

He made the promise with such an outrageous grin that she couldn't hold back an answering chuckle. The laughter felt so good after the storm of emotions she'd experienced last night that she followed it up with the idiocy of climbing on the black-and-chrome beast.

With an order to Wolf to stay, she fumbled for

the footrests and laced her arm around Evan's waist.

It didn't take Lissa long to figure out why mature and otherwise intelligent men like Evan Henderson might prefer a motorcycle over a car as a means of transportation. It was the ultimate male fantasy. Freer than the wind. Faster than sex.

The engine throbbed. Vibrations pulsed through spread legs. The wind tore at clothes. The babe on the back seat had to cling to the driver at every turn…particularly since the babe in question had never ridden a motorcycle in her life.

Evan navigated the sloping path down from the trailer, hit the main road and opened the throttle. Like a racing greyhound released from the gate, the bike leaped forward. It took Lissa a few miles to get used to the noisy rumble of the stock pipes, a few miles more to adjust to the sensation of all that lean, mean machine between her legs.

The feel of his back hard and smooth against her front added considerably to the novel experience. The bike didn't come equipped with a backrest, so Lissa rode with her hips nestled against his and her arms looped around his waist. She could feel every shift in his muscles, every flex of his thighs.

To her surprise, she soon caught the heady sense of power that came with running fast and low to the ground. They rode south, then west on a two-lane county road, the morning sun behind them and the desert ahead. Giant saguaros stood like sentinels on the rolling ridges. Rarer pipe organ cacti dotted the south-facing slopes. Gluttons for heat and light, the pipe organs bloomed mostly at night, but a few still showed their lavender-white petals. Clumps of prickly pear and cholla made a flashy display of their summer blooms, painting the landscape with splashes of brilliant yellow, red, white and orange.

Evan was right, Lissa thought as the wind teased strands of her hair from the helmet and whipped them around her face. The warmth of the sun on her back, the vast emptiness of the desert, the sense that they were alone in the universe…all combined to blow the cobwebs from her mind.

For the moment at least, the past lay behind her in Paradise. The future shimmered somewhere ahead, distant and unseen. The present was right now, right here…with the man who'd argued and bluffed and pushed his way past her defenses.

After a good half hour or more, he throttled down and slowed to a stop at a pull-off with a panoramic overview of the purple-smudged Castle Dome Mountains. Lissa was ready—more than ready—to swing her leg over the seat, remove her helmet and walk beside him on wobbly legs to the iron railing.

A metal sign attached to the railing provided de-

tailed information about the topography and envi-
ronment of the area, but Lissa ignored the rusted
plate. Her concentration centered on Evan. The set
of his shoulders in the wrinkled denim shirt. The
strong, clean line of his jaw. The white lines web-
bing the corners of his eyes.

"What's the verdict?" he asked with a smile.
"Think I can make a biker out of you?"

"I'll let you know when I work the rubber out
of my legs and the squashed bugs out of my skin."

Grinning, he rested his hips against the rail and
reached out to thumb a speck of something off her
cheek.

"You look good in squashed bugs."

"Ugh!" She wrinkled her nose, wet a finger and
scrubbed at the spot. "Did I get it?"

"You got it." Angling his hips, he drew her
between his thighs and treated her face to a long,
lazy scrutiny. "You look good even without bugs,
Lissa."

His hands rested lightly on her waist. She could
feel their weight on the swell of her hip. Feel, too,
the strength in his forearms when she curled her
hands around the lean muscle.

Before last night, she wouldn't have allowed
herself the pleasure of this contact. Before their
ride through the hot, clean desert morning, she
would have eased out of this too-intimate embrace
and put a safe distance between them.

Now, the cobwebs had cleared and she knew she

wanted nothing more of life at this particular moment than his mouth on hers. Taking her courage in both hands, she smiled up at him.

"You look pretty good yourself."

He cocked a brow. "No gnats decorating my chin?"

"No."

"No dust caked in the corners of my eyes?"

"Uh-uh."

"You sure? Maybe you'd better take a closer look."

The husky thread that wove through his voice sent a thrill down her spine. She expected him to draw her into him, fully anticipated that he would nudge her forward another inch or two and bring their bodies into contact. A few seconds passed before she realized he was waiting for her to take the next, gargantuan step.

Her heart in her throat, Lissa slid her palms up his shirtsleeves. Inched closer. Tangled her fingers at the back of his neck.

"I can't see a thing wrong from here."

"Oh, baby," he got out on a half groan, half laugh. "Neither can I."

That was all the encouragement she needed. Rising up with a slither of cotton against denim, she angled her mouth to his. Greed burst in her at the first touch. Pleasure followed, swift and sweet.

She could have lost herself in the kiss. The earth could have spun and the sun blazed down until they were both baked as brown as Josephine's cornflakes casserole and Lissa wouldn't have noticed. It barely registered on her spinning senses when Evan's hands glided down and tugged at the hem of her hot pink top.

While his hands worked their rough magic on her bare back, his mouth traced a line down her throat. She arched her neck, gasping in pleasure as he nipped at the straining cords, then gasped again when his busy hands slid around her ribs to her breasts.

How did he do it? she wondered desperately. How did he flame her skin with just a touch? Ignite needs she hadn't felt in...in...*ever!* They surged upward from deep in her belly, speared into her chest, wild and urgent and all consuming. Lissa's hammering heart beat a desperate message to her brain.

Go for the gold! Just this once.

Let down your guard and grab at that shiny ring.

She wanted to. Sweet heaven above, she wanted to. Shaking with need and nervousness, she cleared her throat.

"Evan."

"Mmm?"

"How fast does the Hawg go?"

His head lifted. "How fast do you want it to go?"

"Can you get us back to Paradise before either

one of us wakes up and realizes how insane this is?''

He went still for three heartbeats, maybe four. Then he scooped her up in his arms, strode back to the bike and plopped her on the rear seat.

''Buckle the helmet and hang on tight, sweetheart. We're gonna smoke some tar.''

Chapter 12

Later, much later, Lissa would admit that she buckled on the helmet nursing the secret belief that the fire in her veins would cool to a reasonable simmer during the long ride back to the trailer. That sanity would return, and she and Evan would both realize how crazy it would be for them to tumble into bed together.

They hardly knew each other! He was a lawyer, for Pete's sake, a life-form she had particular cause to loathe. He zipped in and out of Paradise on a whim, disturbing the peace she'd worked so hard to achieve. On top of that, Lissa still hadn't sorted out her anger and hurt over the news he'd brought her about the man who'd fathered her. The last thing she needed was to complicate her life further by giving in to this insane urge to come apart in Evan's arms.

Unfortunately she severely underestimated the power of anticipation. Hot little needles pierced her the instant she spread her legs and scooted forward. The needles grew to swordlike proportions when road vibrations added their torment to the press of her body against his. Every ripple of his muscles as he leaned into a turn, every flex of his thighs as he shifted in the seat did a separate and distinct number on Lissa's screaming nerves.

By the time he aimed the Harley up to the hill to the trailer, fishtailed to a stop and dodged Wolf to drag her inside, her mind had turned to mush. The way he backed her against the wall and locked his mouth on hers didn't help matters, either. When they finally came up for air, her knees were so wobbly she would have crumpled if she hadn't been propped against the wall.

Eyes lit with blue flames burned into her skin wherever they touched. Her mouth, her throat, the jerky rise and fall of her breasts above the scoop-necked tank top all felt the heat. Planting both palms beside her head, he gave her a wolfish smile.

"You remember Marsh's description of a Saturday Night Special?"

"How could I forget?"

"Want to hear how Reece describes a Friday Morning Delight?"

"Is…?" She swiped her tongue along her swollen lips. "Is today Friday?"

With Evan's breath hot on her cheek and his chest hard against the tips of her breasts, she couldn't remember her name, much less the day of the week.

"You start fast," he told her in a husky whisper. "Up against the wall. Clothes ripped off. Muscles torqued. Bodies sweat slick and hot."

"That sounds…interesting," Lissa said faintly.

"You finish slow. On the floor. Or the couch. Or any other handy horizontal surface. Lots of touching. Tonguing. Tasting."

A glimmer of reason pushed its way through the sensual haze his words evoked. He was giving her the option. Fast, slow or both.

Or neither.

She could feel him rock-hard and straining inside his jeans. Feel his chest muscles quivering against her breasts. He had her caged against the wall and so darned hot for him she was blistering from the inside out. Yet still he was giving her the option.

The last of Lissa's barriers crumpled. She didn't love him. She'd learned the hard way not to fool herself into believing this ache around her heart had anything to do with love. Yet the fact that he would haul her into the trailer like a caveman dragging his prize into his lair, then practically give himself a hernia holding back caused a funny little quiver in her chest.

The need clawing at her throat became a molten, liquid flame. Slowly she slid her hands inside the waistband of his jeans.

"I'll tell you what," she murmured hoarsely. "Let's forget Reece and Marsh's specials." The snap on his jeans gave with a pop. "I'm more interested in your version of things."

Evan's version, she discovered in the following instant, took her straight from semicoherent to lost. Totally, completely lost.

When he flashed her a wicked grin, the power of speech deserted her.

When he buried his hands in her hair and dragged her head back for his kiss, her knees gave out.

And when he followed that tongue-swallowing kiss with a bumpy ride down the hall to the bedroom, she dissolved into helpless giggles.

The narrow hallway wasn't designed to accommodate oversize men transporting medium-size women in their arms. Lissa's knees banged the wall. Evan's shoulders scraped the doorjamb. They got wedged in the doorway for a ridiculous moment before he figured out the right angle to get them both through.

She was still laughing when he dumped her on the bed and stripped off his shirt. Her giggles stuck

in her windpipe, though, when he heeled off his
boots and jeans.

A lump formed in Lissa's throat. Evan fully
clothed and standing stranded in the road had set
off warning alarms all through her body. Evan with
his shirt hanging open and his jeans riding low on
his hips earlier this morning had caused a serious
malfunction in her central nervous system.

But this Evan… This lean, muscled, *naked* Evan
stopped her heart. She barely had time to admire
his awesome symmetry before he planted a knee
on the bed and proceeded to relieve her of her
clothes as well.

He did it with such style, such flair.

Such blinding speed!

Lissa formed the fleeting thought that Evan's
younger brothers had probably taken a few tips
from him in developing their particular specials.
Then his gaze did a slow slide down her body and
she forgot about his brothers, forgot about the specials, forgot everything except the awe in his eyes
when they came back to hers.

"Do you have any idea how beautiful you are?"

Beautiful? With her nose no doubt glowing like
Rudolph's after that wild bike ride, her hair still
damp and sticky from being crammed into the helmet, and goose bumps pickling every inch of her
skin in the chill pouring from the trailer's swamp
cooler?

On second thought, maybe it was the croak in

Evan's voice that raised those tiny bumps. It certainly puckered her nipples into tight, hard points. All Lissa knew was that when he joined her on the bed, she was past caring how she looked.

Within moments, she was past caring about *anything* except the intense, intensifying pleasure it gave her to touch and be touched by him.

The slow, exploring stroke of palms against skin swiftly gained speed and heat. The erotic dance of tongue to tongue gave way to greedy little shoulder and breast and tummy kisses. When Evan traced a wet trail up her body to tease an aching nipple with his mouth and teeth, Lissa's back arched. His hands, his wild, wonderful hands, stroked and kneaded and generally played havoc with every one of her senses.

But she didn't grasp how skillfully he'd primed her until he kneed her legs apart. The first stroke of his thumb against her oversensitized flesh almost sent her into orbit.

"Evan!"

His breath washed hot and damp in her ear. "I'm right here."

He certainly was! He was all over her, his scent, his mouth, his slick, muscled body. Frantic to give him the same maddening pleasure he was giving her, she wedged a hand down his stomach and curled her fingers around his rigid shaft. It filled her hand, hot and hard and already dewed at the tip.

To her satisfaction, her touch produced an instant and electric reaction, just as his had a moment ago. Sucking in a sharp hiss, he went utterly still. Two strokes later, he jerked away.

She saw him dive for the edge of the bed and grope frantically for his jeans. Heard a mumbled curse, then a ripping sound as he tore open a condom. A heartbeat later, he repositioned himself between her thighs.

If Lissa wasn't already coming apart at the seams, the expression on Evan's face at that moment would have unraveled her. There was no sign of the smooth, sophisticated attorney. No evidence he even existed.

Blue eyes burned into hers. His hair was rough where she'd thrust her hands through it. His rugged features were flushed with a desire so intense it singed his cheekbones. Her heart thudded when he gathered her in his arms and crushed his mouth with hers.

He came into her with an easy probe, stretching, filling. Withdrew. Began a rhythm that was soon too slow for either of them. Within moments, they were panting, their bodies slick and hard and straining with a need that engulfed them both.

The explosion that came crashing down took Lissa by surprise. It was so swift, so shattering, she hardly felt her muscles contract, barely registered the searing sensation that gathered at her center before it detonated. She arched her back, thrust her hips up. A groan tore from the back of her throat as the pleasure took her.

Evan stilled, his hands buried in her hair, his body taut on hers. Dimly she heard a hoarse murmur, whether his or her own she wasn't sure. Vaguely she sensed his fierce struggle to wait while she rode the waves. They were still rippling through her when he picked up the rhythm again, only faster, harder.

The swamp cooler was battling a fierce afternoon when Evan took his turn in the Fiberglas coffin that served as Lissa's shower stall. Tepid water dribbled from the single, rusted faucet. The showerhead was set so low he had to poke his backside out the curtain to bend enough to rinse the soap from his upper torso.

Despite his awkward contortions, a fierce satisfaction thrummed in his veins. A hefty measure of that satisfaction stemmed from the three incredible hours he'd just spent in Lissa's bed. Yet, as impossible as it seemed, those hours were only a prelude to the pleasure that now pierced him at the sounds drifting down the hall.

She was in the front room, singing. Or more correctly, humming. Like a playful bird riding a summer breeze, the liquid notes dipped and soared and rippled joyously. It was the first time Evan had heard her sing since the day he'd unin-

tentionally sicced Hawthorne on her. The first time
he'd heard her singing live, anyway.

He'd picked up a half dozen of her CDs in San
Diego and listened to them late at night this past
week. Amplified and backed up by singers and a
band, her clear, ringing voice was a powerful instrument that lingered in his head almost as long
as the image of the woman behind it.

He liked it better like this. Unaccompanied. Un-
amplified. Just Lissa humming out a lilting melody
that could have been a hymn or a love song.

He stopped cold, one foot in the shower stall and
one on the fuzzy pink rug beside it. An odd sensation rippled down his spine. An even odder one
curled in his stomach.

Frowning, Evan grabbed the towel. It was too
soon to think of love. Too soon to think of anything other than when and how he was going to
maneuver Lissa down that narrow hallway into bed
again. He was still trying to convince himself that
constituted his top priority when he joined her in
the living area.

She was at the sink, washing out the breakfast
dishes they'd left on the table hours ago. Her humming cut off abruptly when he appeared, and Evan
needed only one look at the shy smile she aimed
his way to instantly rearrange his priorities. His
number one order of business from this point on
was to find ways to keep a smile on her face.

Which might be a challenge considering the possible heartache that waited for her in LaGrange.

Never one to dodge the inevitable, Evan claimed first a kiss and then the dish towel hanging from a hook beside the sink.

"Since you survived your first experience on a Harley with no noticeable scrapes or bruises, want to take the bike into LaGrange instead of your pickup?"

Her soapy hands stilled for a moment, then swished a sponge vigorously across a plate. "I'm not planning a trip into LaGrange."

"You're going to have to face him sooner or later."

"Says who?"

Yanking the plate from the dishpan, she ran it under the rinse water and plunked it in the drainer. The crockery piece clattered ominously against the others already stacked there. Evan plowed ahead despite the obvious warning.

"Wouldn't you rather know what he wants than sit here and stew about it?"

"I've got a good idea what he wants."

"A piece of Missy Marie?"

"What's left of her, anyway." A fistful of knives and forks landed in the strainer with a jangle of metal. "That's what they all want."

"You want to define 'they'?"

She caught the subtle coolness behind the question and ceased the sponge attack on Josephine's

casserole dish. Her eyes were troubled when they
lifted to his, but she answered with brutal honesty.

"Not you, Evan. I don't think you're one of the
vultures who are still so eager to pick my bones."

"You don't *think* so, huh?" The dish towel
wrapped around a dripping coffee mug. "Let me
know when you're sure, will you?"

Pink crept up her cheeks. "Hey, gimme a break
here. You've pretty well turned my world on its
ear in the past twenty-four hours. I'm still trying
to figure out which end is up."

That was better, Evan decided. Much better.

"Let me know when you figure that out, too,
will you?" he said ruefully.

She looked a little startled at the idea he might
be as confused right now as she was. Setting the
mug aside, he braced his hands on the counter and
bracketed her hips.

"This is all pretty overwhelming to me, too,
Lissa. I didn't expect you to keep me awake almost
every night last week. I didn't plan on coming back
to Paradise. And I sure as heck didn't anticipate
what just happened between us." His mouth
kicked up. "I'd *hoped* for something along those
lines, you understand. But I didn't really believe
my luck until I felt you shudder beneath me."

The pink in her cheeks flamed red. "I'm having
a hard time believing it, too."

"Hmm. Let's see what I can do to make a *gen-
u-ine* believer out of you."

Evan intended it as only a light, teasing kiss. Yet the moment his lips brushed Lissa's, the flame they'd just doused leaped instantly to life again. He jerked his head up, confounded by the heat that stabbed at his groin.

Well, hell! He hadn't counted on this grand slam to the gut every time he touched the woman!

He backed away, fighting something akin to sheer, male panic. Lusting after Lissa and wanting to keep a smile on her face instead of that tight, closed look she too often wore was one thing. This sudden desire to tumble her back into bed and keep her there for the next twenty or thirty years was something else again.

He was slogging through quicksand here, sinking deeper with every step. In the back of his mind he could almost hear his brothers snickering. The last Henderson standing was about to go under.

To allow time for his panic to settle, Evan channeled his thoughts away from the unmade bed at the end of the hall and back to the issue Lissa kept trying to dodge.

"My boss wasn't real happy with me for time off again. I'll have to head back to San Diego tomorrow. You sure you don't want me to ride into LaGrange with you this afternoon and confront your father?"

"No."

"No, you aren't sure, or no, you don't want to?"

"No, I don't want to ride into LaGrange this

afternoon or tomorrow or anytime in the foresee-able future.''

"You can't just ignore the fact that he's there.''

"He abandoned *me,* Evan. I didn't walk out on him.'' Wrapping her hands around her waist, she tried to disguise the hurt in her voice with a steel barb. "He's had plenty of time in the past few weeks to make contact. For whatever reasons of his own, he's chosen not to.''

"We're just assuming he knows who you are,'' Evan reminded her gently. "The law of averages says he didn't turn up in LaGrange by chance, but we can't discount that possibility.''

"I can. I figure he's here for one of two reasons. To try to sell a story about his long-lost little girl to the media or to try for a cut of the money every-one's convinced Doc and I stashed away.''

"Let's talk about that money.'' Abandoning his dish towel, Evan hooked a kitchen chair and strad-dled it. "As I understand the matter, this character Jonah Dawes deposited a little over four million in offshore accounts over a five-year period.''

"Four million, three hundred thousand and sixty-seven dollars, if you want to be exact,'' Lissa said dryly. "Half of that he earned in commissions and from the bonuses he paid himself as my agent/manager. The rest...'' Her shoulders lifted in a shrug she didn't quite pull off. "I've paid back all but a few thousand of the rest.''

"The warrants against Dawes are still outstanding," Evan reminded her. "We could go after him. I got a tip that he may be in Casa Grandes, Mexico, living like some emperor in a mountaintop villa."

He didn't tell her that the tip had come from his brother, who'd called in a few favors owed him by his counterparts south of the border. Or that one of those very accommodating law enforcement officials had generously offered to sidestep the extradition process and deliver the fat-assed gringo, bound and gagged, in the trunk of a car to any spot north of the border Marsh designated.

"I don't care where he's living," Lissa said flatly. "I've put that whole sordid chapter of my past behind me."

"Are you sure?"

"Yes."

"Then why are you still hiding out in Paradise?"

"I'm not hiding. I'm... I'm...living exactly the way I want to," she finished lamely.

"Just out of curiosity, how long do you plan to live 'exactly' like this?"

Her chin tipped. "As long as I can."

She didn't like being pushed. And judging by the way she bristled at the question, Evan figured he wasn't the only one doing the pushing. He'd bet Charley and Josephine had done their share, too.

"So whenever I want to see you," he mused, "I'll have to carve a few days out of my schedule and ride back to Paradise, is that it?"

Her chin went up another notch. "That's it."

He was slogging deeper into the quicksand with every minute. As he pushed out of the chair and took her face between his palms, Evan suspected he might not ever make it back to solid ground.

"Did anyone ever tell you you're one stubborn female, Ms. James?"

A rueful smile came into her eyes. "A good number of people, as a matter of fact."

Chapter 13

"I swear, you're the stubbornest creature the good Lord ever put on this earth."

Josephine followed Lissa around the crowded living room, singing a now-familiar refrain. She'd been delivering variations on the same theme ever since Evan went home to San Diego three days ago.

"Why did you let him get away?"

Lissa drew in a long, patient drag of air heavily scented with nutmeg and cinnamon. Josephine had put one of her mouthwatering cactus pear tortes in the oven right after Lissa's arrival.

"He has a life," she reminded Josephine. The feather duster in her hand flicked along a row of china cats lined atop her friend's hutch. "And a job. He's a big man in the district attorney's office."

"Honey, from what I've seen of him, that man's just plain big all around. You don't find shoulders like that on your everyday average Joe." A wicked smile tipped her peach-tinted lips. "Does the rest of him measure up?"

Lissa maintained a dignified silence, but Jo cackled in delight as a furious blush heated her cheeks.

"You know what they say, don't you?"

"No, and don't think I want to!"

"The bigger they are, sweetie, the harder they fall. You're not the woman I think you are if you can't bring Evan Henderson to his knees."

"First, I'm not sure I want him on his knees. Second..."

A heavily ringed finger flapped in her face. "I don't want to hear any seconds. When's he coming back to Paradise?"

"When—and I'm quoting here—he can carve another few days from his schedule."

The feather duster flicked again. A sleek little Siamese stared at Lissa through green glass eyes. The figurine reminded her all too vividly of the equally sleek and just as feline female who Evan swore he was *not* involved with.

She believed him. The irritating twinge that darted through her at the thought of the two of them working shoulder-to-shoulder fourteen hours a day couldn't be doubt. Or jealousy. Or any of those other annoying emotions that too often accompanied the first flutters of love.

She hadn't fallen in love with Evan. She'd only known him for a few weeks. Spent maybe twenty or thirty hours in his company.

The duster moved to the next shelf. Tiny motes swirled. The row of china cats grinned. Unable to stop herself, Lissa grinned back. She had to admit a good number of those twenty or thirty hours in Evan Henderson's company definitely constituted quality time.

Heat curled through her at the memory of their incredibly erotic session in the easy chair just before he left. She wouldn't have believed the big, scruffy chair could stand up under such energetic, acrobatic use.

Another of Josephine's cackles broke into her private reverie. "You should see the look on your face!"

Instantly Lissa rearranged her features. "What look?"

"You went all gooey-eyed on me. Just thinking about him puts a kink in your tummy, doesn't it?"

Sighing, Lissa gave up the pretense. She didn't have it in her to lie. "Thinking about him definitely puts a kink somewhere. And the feeling scares the heck out of me."

A half-dozen parrot-colored plastic bracelets

clattered as Josephine took her arm and drew her toward the couch. Lissa sank down, still clutching the feather duster. The blue, orange and green jungle design on her friend's sequined T-shirt winked in the afternoon sunlight when she settled beside Lissa.

"Did Evan ask you to go back to San Diego with him?" she asked, her eyes bright behind a double row of sparkling rhinestones. "Or at least come for a visit?"

"Several times."

"Well? What in the world are you hanging around here for? Pack a bag and hit the road, girl."

"You know it's not that simple."

"It's exactly that simple," the older woman retorted. Snatching at the duster, she tossed it aside and took Lissa's hands in both of hers. Her ringed fingers gripped with surprising strength. "You either spend the rest of your life hiding from your past in Paradise, or you decide you want a future and go for it."

"I'm happy with things just the way they are."

Not as happy as she'd been two weeks ago, before she'd stopped to pick up a stranded biker, she admitted silently.

"Rubbish," Jo said tartly. "You need to get out and taste all there is of life...and use the voice God gifted you with to give other folks joy."

"This voice God gifted me with brought too many folks misery instead of joy."

"So you're human? You made a mistake. That doesn't mean you have to punish yourself for the rest of your life. Look at Johnny Cash. You think he doesn't know what he's singing about in 'Folsom Prison Blues'? Or Willie Nelson. He's probably still trying to straighten out his problems with the IRS. Adversity didn't keep either one of them down for long."

Josephine wasn't saying anything Lissa hadn't told herself a hundred times or more. No one was perfect. Everyone, including gospel/country singing stars, messed up. But dread curled in her stomach at the thought of the cameras and microphones that would be thrust at her.

"You don't know what it was like," she said quietly. "What it would be like *again* if I tried to step back into the public eye. The media would rip me to shreds. Rightfully so, considering all that happened. I don't know if I have the strength to face them down again."

"Sure you do." With a brisk *tsk-tsk,* Josephine patted her hand. "If you and Evan Henderson had come up for air long enough to talk while he was here, maybe you wouldn't have to face them alone this time. Just think about that while I check on my cactus pear torte."

Bracelets jangling, she pushed off the sofa and left Lissa thinking.

* * *

She was still thinking when Evan called that evening.

He'd called the night he left, just to let her know he'd made it all the way back to San Diego without encountering any jackrabbits, and every night since. She hadn't yet grown used to the little jolt of pleasure his voice sparked, but his calls had somehow insinuated themselves into the pattern of her evening.

"Hello, Liss."

"Hello, yourself."

"What are you doing?"

"Talking to you," she said dryly.

She could have sworn she heard him smile. It was still hard for her to let down the barriers, but he was learning how to get around them.

"Did you finish 'One-Way Ticket to Paradise'?"

She threw a glance at the sheets of music stacked neatly beside her keyboard. What had started out as a hymn had somehow transformed itself over the past few days into a sappy, sentimental ballad.

"More or less."

"Will you sing it for me when you come to San Diego this weekend?"

"Who said I was coming to San Diego?"

"Well, when I called Josephine a while ago to thank her for the homemade jalapeño jelly she sent me, she sort of hinted you might make the trip if I argued my case with sufficient skill."

It was just curiosity that made her want to hear his arguments. "I'm listening."

"I miss you."

She waited, twisting the phone cord around her wrist

"That's it?" she asked after a long, silent moment. "That's the sum total of your case?"

"Well, if you want hard evidence, there's this nagging need to hear the sound of your voice. Take tonight, for instance. I had to kick everyone out of my office for a few minutes just so I could call you."

Lissa couldn't help wondering if "everyone" included a certain power-packaged female attorney.

"And then there are the bags under my eyes," Evan continued. "I haven't slept in four nights. Every time I stretch out in bed, I see your mouth swollen from my kiss and your body all slick and gleaming with..."

"Okay, okay!" Not for the world would Lissa admit that similar images haunted her. "Enough."

"So are you going to shake off the dust of Paradise for the weekend?"

"I'll..." The cord took another couple of loops around her nervous fingers. "I'll think about it."

Evan hung up a few minutes later, only half aware of the harbor nightscape outside his windows. He'd cracked some recalcitrant witnesses in his time, but Lissa could give any one of them lessons in digging in their heels and hanging tough.

He might as well resign himself to that fact that she'd poke her nose out of her bolt-hole when, and only when, she was ready. Like her, Evan had a pretty good idea of the hazards awaiting her if and when she did. One of her former fans could recognize her. The media could sniff her out. The nightmare she was trying so hard to put behind her could burst into the headlines all over again.

This time, though, the press might just have the real villain in the piece to glom onto. Fierce satisfaction shot through Evan at the thought of the call he'd taken from his brother a few minutes ago.

Marsh, bless his bulldog soul, had just delivered the news that one of his contacts had spotted Jonah "Doc" Dawes in Cuidad Juárez, just across the river from El Paso. Evidently the man had descended from his mountaintop retreat to meet with a "business associate."

Marsh had conducted some business with that particular "associate" himself and hadn't hesitated to lean on him. The nervous banker had agreed to lure Dawes to a meeting place in El Paso. Customs was set to nail the bastard the moment he set foot on this side of the border.

In the meantime, all Evan could do was wait. And hope to heck Lissa would decide to make the drive into San Diego.

He had it bad, he admitted with a shake of his head. Really bad. Imagining his brothers' gleeful reaction to the news the last Henderson had finally bit the dirt, he turned his back on the spectacular nightscape…and froze.

Carrie lounged in the doorway, arms crossed, chin up. A brittle smile tracked across her face.

"I heard you mention Paradise."

Evan could only guess what else she'd heard.

"I suppose you were talking to the blonde I met when I drove out to that hellhole to pick you up. Let me think…what was her name? Lissa James, wasn't it? *Melissa* James?"

He didn't so much as blink an eye. If Carrie was on a fishing expedition, Evan didn't intend to bait her line.

"Did you want something?"

She studied him for a long moment before pushing away from the doorjamb with a jerky movement that lacked her usual feline grace. Her eyes hard, she shook her head.

"No. Not anymore."

Two days later, Lissa sat with both hands locked around the steering wheel of the pickup. The engine rumbled the floorboards beneath her feet. Cool air pumped from the air-conditioning vents, causing the little Kewpie doll dangling from the rearview mirror to dance and shake her tasseled hips.

She could do it, she told herself grimly. She could cut the engine. Climb out of the truck. Walk across the street to the convenience store.

She'd been working up the nerve for this trip into LaGrange ever since Evan's call the other night. However much she balked at it, she had to come to grips with her past before she could let herself think about a future that might or might not include Evan Henderson. And however much she wanted to deny it, her past included Robert Stockton Arlen James.

Knuckles white, she waited until two teenagers finished paying for their gas and drove off. A sickening mix of emotions churned in her stomach as she reached for the door handle.

He looked up when she walked in, a polite expression on his whiskered face. For an instant, just an instant, a muscle twitched in his cheek. Then brown eyes set deep in sunken sockets smiled a welcome.

"Can I help you?"

She hadn't thought any further than this moment. Hadn't worked out a polite way to ask if he'd dumped his daughter in the street outside the South Oklahoma City Baptist Children's Home twenty-four years ago. Thankful that her tiered denim skirt came equipped with deep pockets, Lissa shoved her fists in and decided she didn't owe him polite.

"Are you Arlen James?"

The smile drained from his eyes. Every cord in his neck went taut. "Yes."

"Robert Stockton Arlen James?"

If she'd harbored any doubts at all, the slow leaching of all color from his face would have banished them.

"Yes."

Her nails dug into her palms. "Why are you in LaGrange?"

Below his unshaven chin, his Adam's apple made a slow, torturous slide down and back up his throat. "I just wanted…to know you're okay."

Sure you did, a raw corner of Lissa's mind sneered. Every breath she pulled into her throat lacerated the lining. Her chest ached with a pain she thought she'd banished forever the day she tossed her ragged, one-eyed Pooh Bear in the garbage can.

"A little late with your concern, aren't you? Like maybe, twenty-four years?"

He managed a single nod. "I followed your career, Missy. From your very first album."

Somehow, she wasn't surprised. With a detachment that rose above her inner torment, Lissa searched for some resemblance between this stranger and her hazy image of the father who'd abandoned her. Vaguely she recalled wavy brown hair, not sparse, shaggy gray. And wide shoulders she once rested her cheek against, not the thin, stooped frame before her. And his scent... She'd never forget that blend of Old Spice and cheap whiskey.

"Your songs gave me hope for a few moments...before I lost it again in a bottle." He cleared his throat with a painful rasp. "Then I read about your trial in an old magazine I picked out of a trash can. My heart ached for you."

"Did it?" She was proud of the cool, sardonic arch to her brow.

"That's the day I stopped drinking."

She steeled her heart against the soul-deep regret in his eyes.

"I sat in the gutter, reading that story and knew I had to find you."

She let her silence speak for itself.

"I couldn't..." He swallowed again, his neck muscles straining with the effort. "I couldn't guide you through your younger years, but I thought maybe..." He lifted his arms, let them drop in a helpless gesture. "Maybe I could help you through these troubles."

How? Lissa wondered scornfully. He didn't know her, didn't have even the vaguest idea what made her tick. Why in the world did he think he could help her?

"So you poked through the McNabbs' mail until you found my address?"

"Yes."

The silence spun out, longer this time, lost in the unbreachable chasm that separated them.

"I drive down to Paradise on my days off," he admitted hoarsely. "Mostly I just go straight through town, like I'm on my way to Yuma, then turn around a few hours later and head back to LaGrange. A couple of times, early morning, I parked off in the distance and watched you jog."

So that explained the itchy feeling she'd experienced.

"One evening, I got up the nerve to start up the road up to your trailer, but your dog started howling and I turned tail and ran."

"That seems to be a habit with you."

She meant the comment to bite into his soul, and it did. The little color that had crept back into his face seeped out again, but he didn't look away or try to excuse the inexcusable.

A sigh started deep in Lissa's heart. After all these years, what did it matter? They were strangers, she and this hollow-eyed man. Hurting him wouldn't erase her pain, and would only make a mockery of the love the McNabbs had showered on her.

"What do you want from me?" she asked, deciding to get to the end of this awkward, tawdry scene before the tears stinging the back of her eyes worked their way to the front.

An unutterable sadness filled his face. "Nothing, Missy."

No! She wouldn't feel sorry for him! "Good! Because I don't have anything to…"

The jangle of the phone cut through her terse reply. The stranger—she couldn't bring herself to think of him as her father—let it ring. Twice. Three times. Until the discordant jangle scraped Lissa's nerves raw and unshed tears burned her eyes.

"Answer it," she muttered, whirling. "I've got to go to the ladies' room."

She brushed past potato chips and cheese snacks, heading for the door tucked between the milk cooler and the coffee machine.

"Yeah, this is Arlen," she heard the man behind the counter acknowledge. "Who's this?"

Her hand was on the doorknob when a familiar name pierced her whirling thoughts.

"Hawthorne? I don't know any Hawthorne."

Lissa froze. Her gaze cut back to the shaggy-haired stranger holding the phone. A frown sliced into his brow as he listened for a moment.

"Why would someone from the San Diego D.A.'s office give my name to a TV reporter?" he asked slowly.

The answer spread disbelief across his face.

"Are you serious? You'll pay me ten thousand dollars? Just to fill you in on Missy Marie's troubled childhood?"

Chapter 14

One shoulder propped against the doorjamb of Lissa's tiny bedroom, Evan surveyed the chaos. Clothes were strewn across every horizontal surface. Cardboard boxes crowded the bed and most of the available floor space.

It was late, long past midnight. Evan still wore the road grit and windburn from his wild ride through the night. He hadn't wasted any time after he'd listened to Charlie's phone message. Hadn't even bothered to track Carrie Northcutt down and confront her. He'd find out whether she was the one who'd contacted Dave Hawthorne when he got back. Right now, his primary concern—his only concern—was Lissa.

"I'll say it one more time," he told her. "I didn't give your father's name to that reporter."

"I believe you."

She didn't act as though she did. Yanking out the bottom drawer of the built-in dresser, she dumped its contents into a box. She'd been like this since Evan arrived fifteen minutes ago. Driven. Determined. Withdrawn, as if she'd already shaken the dust of Paradise from her heels...and him along with it.

"Just out of curiosity, were you planning to call me before or after you hit the road?"

The dresser drawer jammed back into place. She stared at its scarred fiberboard front for several seconds before slowly pushing to her feet. Her eyes found his across the jumble on the bed.

"I hadn't planned on calling you at all."

The barriers were back up, so thick and prickly a less determined man would need a chain saw to get through them. Evan wasn't packing a chain saw, only an iron will every bit as stubborn as hers. He let a hint of it show in the steel underlying his lazy reply.

"That's kind of the way I figured it, too."

A flush climbed her throat. Her chin tipped up in defiance...or was it desperation? She kept the width of the bed between them, maintaining a physical as well as emotional distance.

Evan hadn't touched her since she'd opened the door, then quickly backed away from him. He'd make up for that serious error in judgment in a bit. First, she had to deliver the speech she'd obviously been rehearsing in her head for the past ten minutes. Dragging in a deep breath, she plunged into it.

"Look, we both got a little carried away the last time you were here."

"A little?"

"Okay, a lot. It was crazy. The whole weekend was crazy. I knew nothing could come of it… That we couldn't…"

He wasn't letting her off the hook. Weaving a path through the boxes, he came around the end of the bed. Whatever she wanted to say, she'd have to say it right in his face.

"That we couldn't what, Lissa?"

"That we couldn't have any kind of relationship…outside of the hours you could 'carve' out of your schedule."

"Why not?"

"Don't play games with me! You know why not."

"Humor me," he fired back. "Let's hear your version of the facts as you see them."

Goaded, she lifted her chin another notch. "One, there's the *fact* that I've got a past hanging over me that isn't going to go away, no matter how much I wish it. The same black cloud will hang over anyone stupid enough to linger in my general vicinity. Two, there's the *fact* that the cloud's about to burst. My, uh, fath…''

She tripped over the word. Couldn't get it out. Evan's anger melted as she fumbled for a neutral reference to the stranger who'd fathered her.

''Arlen tried to fob Hawthorne off,'' she said tightly, ''but he's probably on his way out here as we speak.''

''We'll handle Hawthorne.''

''Yes, well, you've just hit on *fact* number three. There is no 'we.' There can't be.''

''You're right back where you started. Give it up, Lissa. You've lost this case.''

Surrendering to the need to touch her, he reached out to tuck a strand of her hair behind her ear. She jerked away, desperate now.

''Evan, think! That day, outside Charlie's, Carrie said you're the front-runner for an appointment to the D.A.'s job next year. What do you suppose it will do to your chances if word leaks out that you're tangled up with…someone like me?''

''Ask me if I care about the D.A.'s job.''

''Well, if you don't, I do! I ruined my reputation. I'm not going to ruin yours, too.''

Her jaw set, she tried to wedge past him. Evan's arm shot out. Planting his palm against the wall, he trapped her in the narrow space between the bed and the ancient pecan paneling.

''Ask me if I care about my reputation, Lissa.

And while you're at it, ask me if there's anyone I'd *rather* get tangled up with than you.''

''I'm not going to play word games.'' She gathered her dignity around her like a threadbare coat. ''This is too impor…''

''I love you.''

''Excuse me?''

''I love you.''

Stunned, she stared up at him for long moments. Evan kept one palm hard against the wall and curled the fingers of his other hand under her chin. Gently he nudged up her sagging jaw.

''I know. I'm as flabbergasted as you are.''

Sometime during the wild ride back to Paradise, he'd admitted the truth. Those long, dark stretches of interstate had helped put things in perspective. Or maybe it was his driving need to get to Lissa before she packed up and disappeared.

He would have gone after her, of course, but just the thought that she might disappear for the days or weeks it would take him to find her had generated a wave of urgency. He had to tell her she filled his every thought, every corner of his heart. Had to know if he figured in hers.

''I'm not sure when it happened,'' he admitted, pushing a grin through the tight knot in his throat. ''Sometime between that Saturday Night Special and Friday Morning Delight, I imagine. I just know when Charlie called and relayed the details of your trip into LaGrange this afternoon, I couldn't let you leave Paradise without telling you that I'll go with you. Whenever you choose to leave. Wherever you choose to go.''

''You say that now!'' she cried. ''But you can't imagine what it will be like when the Hawthornes of the world catch up with us.''

''I told you.'' The hand under her chin came up to cup her cheek. ''We can handle Hawthorne and his kind.''

He started to tell her then that he'd already lined up a another juicy story for the persistent reporter. One that would divert the media's attention from Lissa to another, more appropriate prey.

It looked like the pressure Marsh and his Mexican contacts had exerted on Jonah Dawes's ''business associate'' in Cuidad Juárez would soon pay off. As promised, the nervous Mexican banker had set up a meeting with an American counterpart who'd supposedly agreed to funnel Doc's cash reserves into the stock market. The moment Dawes drove across the Rio Grande to the clandestine meeting, a swarm of U.S. Customs officers would descend on his vehicle.

Lissa didn't give Evan the chance to tell her anything about the bust, however. Before his startled eyes, she burst into tears. Feeling as helpless as he did the last time her defenses had crumbled like this, he gathered her in his arms.

''It's okay, Lissa. We'll work this out.''

Clumsily he stroked her hair and waited until

she choked back her sobs and lifted a face at once exasperated and chagrined.

"This is so embarrassing," she sniffled. "I never cry! Never! Why do I keep making such a fool of myself in front of you?"

"Maybe the whole idea of being in love scares you as much as it did me."

She leaned back in his arms to search his face with tear-sheened eyes. "You're scared?"

"Like you wouldn't believe. But you know what they say."

She made a little noise that could have been a sob or a gulp. "The bigger they are..." she murmured raggedly.

"Huh?"

"Never mind. It was just something Josephine mentioned the other day. What do they say, Evan?"

"The best way to conquer your fears is to face them head-on."

She bit down on her lower lip again. Lashes spiked by tears framed wide, questioning eyes.

They'd reached a turning point. They both knew it. Evan had already taken the first step. The next was Lissa's. She could run from her past...and from the future he was offering. Or she could face them both head-on.

Evan didn't realize he'd held his breath until she slid her arms around his neck. Rising up on tiptoe, she brought her mouth within a whisper of his.

"All right. I'm... I'm willing to give it a shot if you are."

It wasn't quite the declaration he'd hoped for, but the way her body melted against his more than made up for the hesitant response.

Despite the smoky love songs she used to croon, Lissa didn't consider herself particularly romantic. She'd never really thought about the appropriate setting for the first time she admitted that she loved and was loved in return. If she had, she probably would have envisioned soft music, dim lights and chilled wine somewhere in the vicinity.

Certainly not a ramshackle trailer. A tiny bedroom so crowded with boxes she couldn't move for fear of planting a foot in one. Or a man who crushed his mouth to hers and fired her with such instant, explosive need that mere moments later she found herself on the floor, wedged between the cartons.

Would it always be like this? she wondered on a gasp as his mouth and teeth worked their rough, tender torment. Would she always flare white-hot at his touch? Always feel this tightening in her womb when she slid her palms along his ridged muscles and smooth, slick flesh? Always tangle her legs around his, and arch her hips to meet his thrusts, and take him into her so greedily?

Would she always look up into his eyes and see herself reflected in their depths?

* * *

Lissa woke first. A combination of refrigerated air and desert dawn chilled her front. Her back snuggled warm and toasty against Evan. Moving slowly so as not to disturb him, she tugged the tangled bedspread free of the box that anchored it and covered them both.

Despite her cautious movements, Evan grunted and shifted his hips. His arm flopped over her waist and lay heavy against the underside of her breast. She trailed a finger along the light furring on his forearm, not wanting to wake him. Only to touch him.

The intensity of this need for contact staggered her. After their explosive joining amid the boxes—and the slower, sweeter coming together that followed—she would have thought her satiated senses couldn't absorb any more of Evan Henderson.

Yet, here she was, lying still and silent in the first pink of dawn, aching all over with the pleasure of just touching him. And worrying more with every featherlight stroke.

Evan had sounded so sure, so confident he could handle the havoc she'd wreak on his career. Maybe he could. The question was, could she?

Her stomach clenched. Although he'd shrugged aside the prospect, she knew she'd destroy his future the way she'd destroyed her own. Overwhelmed with the knowledge, Lissa edged his arm aside and inched off the bed. She had to get outside. Clear her head. Think things through without

the distraction of Evan's all-too-persuasive presence.

Digging through a packed box, she found clean
panties and her white cotton/spandex sports bra.
Tugging on shorts and a top, she searched for her
running shoes. One turned up in a box, the other
under the bed. Sneakers in hand, she tiptoed down
the hall.

Cool, dry air wrapped around her the moment
she stepped outside. The eastern sky wore its
morning dress of riotous pinks and purples. The
sun peeked over the distant mountains and shed
enough light to paint the desert with misty blues
and golds, but not enough to raise the heat waves
that would come later.

While she sat on the top step to pull on her
shoes, a scraggly shadow emerged from under the
trailer, stretching first one leg behind him, then the
other. Instantly another worry pinged at Lissa.
What would she do with Wolf if she went back to
San Diego with Evan, as he wanted her to? He and
the dog had achieved a wary sort of truce, but she
couldn't imagine them living in close proximity,
let alone in Evan's high-rise condo.

"Hello, boy," she said softly, wishing this business of being in love wasn't so darned compli-
cated. "Want to run with me?"

His flanks quivered in anticipation of their morning ritual. Lissa did some quick stretches, then
started off at a slow jog for the path atop the ridge.

Wolf raced ahead, nimbly dodging clumps of prickly pear. He stopped to sniff out his favorite rabbit holes, lifted his leg a few times and doubled back once or twice to make sure Lissa was still slogging along at her usual pace.

On either side of the high ridge, the vast Sonoran Desert stretched to the horizon. Tumbleweeds gleamed a silver-gray in the clear light. A large organ pipe cactus was just folding its tender lavender-white blossoms away for the day. The sky promised another panorama of lucent blue.

The awesome majesty helped Lissa put things in perspective. Bit by bit, the tranquillity of the scene nudged aside everything but the memory of Evan's voice when he'd admitted that he was scared, too. A reluctant smile pulled at her lips. With six feet two of solid muscle and a grin that could make grown women walk into walls, she suspected he'd exaggerated his fears a bit for her benefit.

The sight of a vehicle parked alongside the road some miles outside Paradise snapped the smile off her face. Lissa jerked to a halt, her chest heaving, and stared down from her lofty perspective at the distant car. She didn't have any doubt now about who sat behind the wheel.

Arlen had fobbed Hawthorne off yesterday, fiercely denying that his long-lost daughter lived just ten miles away. But Lissa had seen his jaw drop, and heard the incredulity in his voice when he repeated the reporter's offer. He'd refused, but the disbelief had lingered in his sunken eyes after he'd hung up.

Lissa hadn't been able to take any more at that point. She'd turned on her heel, swept out of the store, and driven home with both shaking hands wrapped around the wheel.

Now that the shock had passed, she supposed she owed him for his attempt to shield her. Assuming, of course, he hadn't snatched up the phone and called Hawthorne back the moment she'd driven off.

One more worry, she thought on a sigh. One more complication.

She'd tell him she was leaving Paradise, she decided. That's all she owed him. Nothing more.

That was her intent, anyway. She hadn't counted on Wolf racing back at the precise moment she decided to make her way down the steep slope to the road below. In joyous pursuit of a scurrying mouse, the dog careened along the narrow trail. The mouse darted between her tennis shoes. Lissa jumped back at the same instant Wolf swerved to miss her. They both went down with a yelp and tumbled off the ridge.

The dog scrambled upright after only a few twisting flips. Far less agile than her four-footed companion, Lissa slid down the rocky slope.

Her arms and legs flailed wildly, scraping against sand and shale. One elbow smashed into something hard. By some miracle, she missed the clumps of cactus dotting the slope, but rolled over several scratchy tumbleweeds. At last she thumped into a shallow-depression and halted her precipitous descent.

Wheezing, she sprawled faceup. She couldn't catch her breath, couldn't feel anything except a stabbing pain in her hip. The overhead sun blinded her. A melange of sounds assaulted her, foremost among them the clatter of stones from the small avalanche she'd started. When the last of the rocks slid past her, the other noises sorted themselves out.

Vaguely she heard Wolf scrabbling down the slope above her, whining in distress. In the distance, a car door slammed and someone—Arlen—shouted her name. As he pounded toward her, Lissa gave serious consideration to letting loose with a shout or a whine herself. At the very least a whimper.

But another sound pierced her eardrums at that moment and paralyzed every one of her muscles, including those in her throat. It was a rattle. A furious rattle.

Only feet from her ear.

Terror suspended all thought. All movement. Lissa didn't breathe. Didn't turn her head. Didn't *want* to turn her head! She wasn't into snakes at the best of times, and definitely not when one was shaking his tail right beside her ear.

"Missy!" Footsteps thudded across the desert floor. "Sweet Lord, Missy, don't move!"

She barely heard the frantic shout. Everything she'd ever heard, everything she'd read about rattlesnakes since she'd moved to Paradise thundered in her head. Snakes were defensive animals. They'd go to any lengths to avoid contact. When provoked or startled, they'd take flight and only attack if there was no way out.

Even if they did attack, there was always the chance they'd just fed, just drained their reservoir of venom to stun another prey. She managed one choked prayer that this particular rattler had gorged itself silly right before Lissa tumbled off the ridge and into its nest.

She'd never know what told her the reptile was about to strike. Maybe it was the sudden hiss almost buried amid the furious rattles. Or the snarl that ripped from Wolf's throat as he launched himself down the rest of the slope. Or the sixth sense all creatures exhibit in the face of danger.

Instinct had her flinging up an arm to protect her face.

Instinct brought Wolf flying across her body, teeth bared.

Instinct sent her father into a crashing dive a half second before the rattler struck.

Chapter 15

For the rest of her life, Lissa would shudder every time she recalled the horrific moments that followed her tumble down the slope.

Man, dog and snake convulsed in a blur of whirling, writhing movement. Wolf's savage snarls ripped through air that vibrated with furious hisses and rattles.

Terrified, Lissa rolled onto her side and scrabbled frantically to her hands and knees. Choking with horror, she saw Wolf emerge from the melee, his jaws locked behind the head of a slashing, gray-brown diamondback.

It couldn't have taken the dog more than a few seconds to finish off the creature. But every snarl that ripped from his throat, every vicious spin of his body, every time he slammed the rattler's scaly length against the ground, stopped Lissa's heart.

With a final jump and midair twist, Wolf flipped the carcass over his back and—mercifully—out of sight. Legs spread, ears back, fangs bared, he swung his head from side to side, searching for other foe.

His feral growls beat the air as Lissa crawled the few feet to the third combatant in the deadly duel. Fear contorting his haggard face, Arlen pushed himself up on one elbow.

"Missy! Baby, did it bite you?"

"I don't..." She lifted a shaky hand, shoved back her bangs. "I don't think so."

"Are you sure?"

A quick visual showed a considerable collection of scrapes and cuts but nothing resembling fang marks.

"I'm okay."

"Thank God!"

He crumpled back to the ground, his eyes closing.

"What about you?" she asked on a wave of panic. "Did it get you?"

His lids fluttered up. A slow apology filled his eyes. "'Fraid so."

"Oh, God! Where?"

He lifted his left arm an inch or two and gestured to his right. Lissa's lungs squeezed when she spotted the small, diagonal wound just below a tattooed eagle.

"Don't fret," he said hoarsely. "You're all right. That's all that matters to me."

"Not to me!"

Throwing back her head, she gulped down her panic. Okay! All right! She'd made it a point to read up on the desert when she first moved to Paradise. Picked up all kinds of information about kangaroo rats and Gila monsters and sidewinders...including several articles on ways to prevent and treat venomous bites.

One in particular her frantic brain dredged up. It was written by Rattlesnake Ray, who claimed the dubious distinction of stuffing more venomous pit vipers into a burlap bag than any other living Texan. Among other things, the article stressed that some eight thousand people were bitten every year in the United States. Maybe nine or ten died. Lissa latched onto that statistic like a drowning swimmer would a lifeline.

Only then did she recall that article also stressed the need to stay calm and analyze the situation.

Calm! With her father stretched out on the ground, venom seeping into his veins! Gritting her teeth, she forced the tremors from her voice.

"I'm trying to remember what I read about snakebites. I'm pretty clear on what *not* to do."

A half smile, half grimace tracked across his haggard face. "I'm all ears, Missy-mine."

Somewhere under her layers of near panic, a memory clicked. He'd called her that. Missy-mine. When he rocked her to sleep.

She couldn't think about that now! Couldn't think about anything except those *don't do's.*

"You can't move, okay? No walking or running or anything to speed up your circulation. And no tourniquets, just a…a pressure bandage."

Her thoughts whirling, she'd reached out to tear a strip off his shirt when she realized she had something that would work much better. Yanking the hem of her tank top free of her jeans, she ducked her arms inside and jerked them though the straps of her sports bra. The stretchy fabric would constrict as well as an Ace bandage.

"Just lie still. Keep your arm low, below the level of your heart if possible. I'll wrap this right here, above your elbow."

Her hands shaky, she rolled up his sleeve. The oozing puncture wound in his arm raised a sob in her throat. Fiercely Lissa choked it back.

When she had the spandex wrapped around his upper arm just above the wound, she sat back on her heels and tried frantically to remember what came next. Most of the articles said not to cut into the wound or try to suck out the venom by mouth. They recommended instead use of the little rubber suction pump that came with commercial snakebite kits. Which was all well and good if you happened to have one of those suckers handy!

Swallowing hard, Lissa eyed the blood trickling down her father's arm. She suspected that the caution against sucking the venom out stemmed in part from worry over transmission of diseases like AIDS. Seeing that thin, crimson line brought that worry slamming home.

She didn't know the man whose blood dripped onto the sand. Had no idea where he'd been for the last twenty years, or what caused his hollow-cheeked gauntness. As quickly as those grim thoughts flashed into Lissa's mind, she shoved them aside.

She couldn't let him die. She couldn't let anyone die.

"I'm going to try to get the venom out. Just lie still."

"I'm not goin' anywhere," he said with a feeble smile.

Returning his smile with a wobbly one of her own, she bent over his arm. With the first suck, the coppery taste of blood filled her mouth. She spat it out and sucked again.

Within moments, the small wound had yielded all the liquid it would. Clearing her mouth as best she could of the residue, Lissa dragged in a deep breath while she considered her next options.

Getting medical help was right up there at the top of the list. So was watching the victim for signs of swelling or shock or convulsions leading to possible cardiac arrest. If the worst happened, she'd have to administer CPR. How could she do that if she had to seek help?

With the wild idea of trying to roll him onto her back and carry him to the car, she swiveled on her heels to gauge the distance to the parked vehicle. Harsh reality killed that idea instantly. She'd never be able to stagger that far without jostling him and doing far more harm than good. Gulping, she made a wrenching decision.

"I've got to go for help." Her hand fluttered down to cover his. "I'll take your car. It's only a few miles to my trailer. Evan's there. We'll call 911 and come right back. I swear."

His eyes gentled at her obvious distress. "I know you will."

She tried to get her feet under her. Told herself she had to leave him. Yet the possibility that he might die alone under the now blazing sun kept her in place.

"Don't look so scared, baby."

He turned his hand, just an inch or two and wove his fingers through hers. Lissa trembled at the contact.

"I've been trying to kill myself the hard way ever since your mother died. If all the poison I poured down my throat over the years didn't finish me off, this little bit won't do the job, either."

She nodded, unable to speak.

He searched her face, from her scraped forehead

to her chin, as if to imprint her features on his mind for all eternity.

"I'm so sorry for those wasted years, Missy. So sorry I left you. I love you. I've always loved you. I just couldn't..." His Adam's apple worked. "Couldn't..."

"We'll talk about that later," she promised fiercely. "When I get back."

With a last, gentle squeeze of her hand, she pushed off her heels. She'd taken only a step when she remembered Wolf. She spun around, relieved to see him on his feet and watching her with his usual wary alertness. Apparently the snake had emptied its venom in the man before the dog attacked.

Wolf could stand watch over her father until she got back.

"Stay here, boy! Sit!"

He made a small whine of protest.

"Sit!"

Clearly unhappy, he sank onto his haunches.

"Okay, now stay! Stay, Wolf, stay!"

With that gruff order, she spun around and took off. She could only hope that whoever had owned him before losing him to the desert had drilled the command into him.

Her heart pounding, she flew across rock-strewn terrain. Despite the urgency that grabbed at her throat, she kept a wary eye on the ground ahead. She couldn't help her father if she put her foot down on another rattler. With every step, she poured her terror into prayer.

She was halfway to the parked car when a distant roar cut through the now smothering heat of the desert. Lissa whipped her head around, yelping with joy when a helmeted figure on a black-and-silver behemoth rose through the shimmering heat waves.

"Evan!"

The little blip of worry Evan had experienced a half hour ago when he woke to find Lissa gone didn't begin to compare to the fear that knifed through him when she stumbled onto the road ahead of him.

Then, it had only taken a quick glance out the trailer's window to see that she hadn't succumbed to a fresh attack of nerves and bolted. Her rusted pickup was still parked next to his bike.

Now, her wildly waving arms and frantic face told him something had spooked her, and bad. But not until he'd started to throttle back did Evan see the bloody scrapes on her face and legs. Rubber screamed on asphalt as he wrenched the handlebars around and skidded to a stop.

She ran at him, her words lost in the dying roar of the engine.

"Lissa, what...?"

"It's my father! A rattlesnake bit him. He's over there! With Wolf!"

Evan followed the line of her outflung arm, saw a dark shadow against the sand that looked like her scruffy pet.

"Get on!"

Waiting only until he felt her arms lock around him, he opened the throttle. The Harley bucked once, bit dirt, then raised a plume of dust as it raced across the desert. Evan was off the bike and down on one knee beside the fallen man before the dust settled.

"I wrapped the bandage around him right away," Lissa panted, hanging over his shoulder. "Then sucked out what I could."

Nodding, Evan met the older man's intent gaze. "Do you feel any burning?"

"A little."

"How high up does it go?"

Arlen held his eyes. If he didn't know, he could probably guess the implications behind the quiet question. The further the burning sensation had traveled, the greater the likelihood the venom would damage his heart and central nervous system.

"It only stings below my elbow right now. Lissa kept me still and went right to work."

"Smart woman, your daughter."

"Smart...and kind," he murmured, his glance drifting over Evan's shoulder. "Like her mother."

"I'll take your word for that."

Gently, he probed the flesh around the wound. To his relief, he detected only slight swelling.

He'd lost enough horses to rattlesnake bites during his boyhood years on the Bar-H to know the signs. A rapid swelling around the wound was usually the second step in sometimes irreversible tissue damage. A lot depended on the size and the species of the creature that had inflicted the bite. Angling around on his heel, he searched the immediate vicinity.

"Anyone get a good look at the snake? Note its size or the arrangements of the bands on its tail?"

"Not me," Arlen muttered.

Shuddering, Lissa shook her head. "Me, neither. But it's over there," she added with a grimace. "What's left of it."

"The docs will need to see it to determine whether to administer antivenin."

Stripping off his shirt, Evan strode over to the mangled remains. The broad black and white rings circling its tail identified it as a Western Diamondback. A young one, thank God. In Texas, where rodents were plentiful, these coon-tail rattlers grew to seven or more feet and packed enough venom to take down a bull elephant. Here in Arizona, where the desert took its toll on predator and prey alike, they averaged only about four feet. This one was just under three.

Scooping the carcass up in his shirt, Evan had a

quiet word of praise for the hound that had obviously torn the rattler apart.

"Good boy."

Wolf's gums lifted. A throaty growl rolled up from his chest as he eyed the suspicious bundle. Lissa exhibited a similar response when Evan approached her.

"Sorry, sweetheart. You'll have to carry this. I'll carry your father."

Her mouth twisted, but she took the grisly object without flinching.

"Okay, Arlen." Stooping, Evan slid one arm under the older man's back, the other under his knees. "Let's get you out of this sun and into a hospital."

He surged to his feet with a single flex of his thighs and strode through the scrub toward the car. Lissa hurried after them, the dead snake held out at arm's length and Wolf padding alongside her.

The next hours passed in a blur of knuckle-cracking tension.

Once at the car, Evan laid Arlen across the back seat, making sure to keep his injured arm lowered. Wolf scrunched down at Lissa's feet in the front seat. The moment the door slammed, Evan pushed the accelerator to the floor to get them back to Paradise.

To Lissa, it seemed like an eternity before they tore into Charlie's Place, tires screaming, but the ride probably didn't take more than five or ten minutes. While Evan ran inside to use the phone, she leaned over the front seat and watched her father for signs of shock. His color remained good, thank the Lord, although his forearm had begun to swell. From the way he chewed hard on his lower lip, she guessed the burning sensation had progressed to severe pain.

She counted the seconds until Evan came tearing out of Charlie's Place with the mechanic following hard on his heels.

"EMS is scrambling a chopper," he told father and daughter. "It'll take them a half hour to get here. How're you doing, Arlen?"

"Hanging in there."

"Good! This should help the swelling."

Hunkering down beside the open car door, Evan wrapped the wet towel around the distended area. That done, he draped his wrists over his bent knees.

"Charlie keeps a stock of snakebite kits in his store, but the paramedics said not to administer the antivenin unless you get dizzy or your vision starts to blur."

What they'd said was that the antivenin could sometimes produce as many complications as the bite itself, including a potentially fatal allergic condition called anaphylactic shock. Evan didn't think either the victim or his daughter needed that bit of information at this point.

"They did suggest electroshock treatment of the injured area. It's a new, supposedly more effective method of stopping the venom's spread. The paramedics told me how to administer it...if you feel up to it."

Arlen lifted a grizzled brow. "You know anything about electricity?"

"My brother's got degrees in both civil and hydroelectric engineering," Evan replied, forcing a grin. "A little of the knowledge he crammed into his head had to have rubbed off on me."

The older man's gaze sought Lissa's. "What do you think, Missy-mine?"

"I think you can trust him," she said with a gulp. "I do."

Evan hurried to gather the necessary equipment, hoping to hell he hadn't gained Lissa's trust only to destroy it by bungling this job. The procedure the medics had outlined sounded pretty straightforward. He'd need about 100K of DC voltage, coupled with amps at about the one or two level. Any coil-based gasoline engine could provide the necessary combination. According to the paramedics, lawnmowers, outboard boat motors, or car engines could be pressed into service.

With Charlie's help, Evan quickly connected a voltage regular to the car's engine, peeled back the ends of an electrical wire and connected one end to the regulator. He was sweating bullets when he hunkered down beside Arlen again.

"The idea is to hit the area with enough voltage to destroy the venom's molecular structure, but not so much it will cause tissue damage or burn your skin."

It sounded good…in theory. With the live wire only inches from Arlen's arm, however, theory was smacking up hard against reality.

"Ready?"

"'Spose so."

"Okay, here we go."

His jaw tight, Evan tapped the exposed end of the wire against the swollen skin an inch or so from the puncture. He allowed only a flick, less than a second of contact. Relief speared through him when Arlen didn't jerk or cry out.

"I'm going to work around the wound in a circular pattern," he told the patient. "Five or six taps. Then we wait ten minutes and do it again, further out. Just lie back. Try not to clench your muscles."

Every moment of that agonizingly slow procedure would remain etched in Lissa's mind forever. Air-conditioning poured from the car's vents. Heat crawled in through the open rear door. She knelt in the front seat. Evan was wedged in the space between the back seat and the door, his jaw tight and brows creased in fierce concentration.

She was cursing her own helplessness when her father's sunken eyes found hers. The plea in them stripped her soul bare.

"Sing to me, Missy. I'd like to hear you sing once before... I'd like to just hear you once."

Her throat ached so badly she didn't think she could force out anything remotely resembling a note. She wet her lips. Swallowed. Reached deep inside her.

"I shall..."

Her voice cracked. She dragged in a breath. Tried again. Softly. Slowly.

"I shall walk...in the light,
I shall sit...in the splendor,
When I come to the Father,
When I find my way to Thee."

By the time the distant beat of a helicopter reached the small group huddled around the dusty car, the hymn carried clear and silver-bright through the heat waves rising from the deserted streets of Paradise.

Chapter 16

Her nerves as brittle as spun glass, Lissa peered through the second-story casement window at the mob jostling for position on the flagstone patio below.

She couldn't believe only four days had passed since those terrifying hours in the desert. Three since the doctors had confirmed that Lissa's on-the-spot first aid and Evan's electroshock treatments had saved Arlen's arm and most likely his life. A mere twenty-four hours since Lieutenant Colonel Sam Henderson had flown a twin-engine Commanche into Phoenix and whisked brother, father, daughter and dog to the Bar-H.

Yet already they'd found her. The reporters, the

reps from the talk shows, the fans. Already the media had converged on Flagstaff, bombarding the folks at the Bar-H with so many calls and requests for interviews that Lissa had agreed to a press conference just to give the Hendersons some peace.

Evan was the one who suggested that she do it here, on safe ground, with his family and hers beside her. He'd also put out the call to the rest of the Hendersons.

They'd responded immediately, converging on the ranch en masse. So many had arrived in the past twenty-four hours, Lissa had trouble sorting them all out. There was Evan's mother, Jess, trim, tanned and proud of the character lines that came from raising five sons. Sam and his wife, Molly, with bright-eyed Kasey darting joyously from uncle to uncle demanding kisses. Dark, handsome Reece and his very talented, very pregnant wife, Sydney. The newest Henderson bride, Lauren, a willowy artist with a shock of glorious auburn hair and a smile that welcomed Lissa warmly.

And Jake. The oldest. The quietest. The saddest.

Strange how Arlen seemed to sense something in Jake, something only the older man could relate to. Last night, while the rest of the family had clustered around the scrubbed oak kitchen table and overwhelmed Lissa with their unquestioned acceptance of her and her past, Jake had spent hours sitting out on the patio with Arlen. They'd talked in quiet stretches. Watched the sun sink behind the

San Franciscos. Listened to the crickets chirp their evening song. With his swollen arm still brutally painful and showing black, necrotic flesh around the wound, Arlen couldn't manage much more.

Somewhat to Lissa's amazement, even Wolf seemed content to simply rest his muzzle on his front paws and lie on the flagstones between the two men. Evan had watched the scene with intense satisfaction, keeping the others away and saying only that it was good for Jake to understand what Arlen had put himself through these past twenty years.

The only Henderson missing from the scene was Marsh, the middle brother. According to Lauren, he'd gotten a call at the airport in El Paso yesterday afternoon, just before they were supposed to board their flight to Arizona. Some hot drug bust or border operation was going down, she'd said with a shake of her head.

They expected him at any minute, though. He'd called an hour ago from twenty thousand feet up, told them to hold the show until he got there. The Henderson brothers would stand shoulder-to-shoulder behind Lissa when she walked out on the patio to face the media.

Dread shivered through her as she gazed down at hastily erected light scaffolding and banks of cameras. The moment she'd tried to avoid for so long had finally caught up with her. Missy Marie's return to the public eye.

She could already hear the questions. The accusations. The demands to know where she'd been for the past three years. The eagerness to learn what she and Doc had done with all the money they'd ripped off.

She could hear, too, the avid curiosity about why she'd chosen to stage her reemergence at the Bar-H, with an assistant U.S. district attorney at her shoulder.

Her wire-tight nerves stretched another torturous notch. This would ruin Evan. The media would have a field day with the fact that one of the government's hottest young prosecuting attorneys was involved with a criminal. Lissa cringed every time she pictured the gleeful headlines that would splash across the tabloids.

She'd thought about denying their relationship, but she suspected neither the media nor Evan would let her get away with that. He certainly hadn't tried to hide how he felt from his family. If they'd had any doubts last night, the casually possessive kiss he'd greeted Lissa with this morning when she stumbled into the crowded kitchen for coffee would have banished them.

Lissa latched onto the memory of that kiss to keep from thinking about the ordeal ahead. She was still reliving it when Evan rapped on the open door. His smile reached out and wrapped her in understanding and a love that kicked the crowd downstairs right out of her mind.

"Ready to face the music?"

"As ready as I'll ever be, I guess."

"You look terrific," he murmured, his eyes gleaming as he took in the costume she'd chosen for Missy Marie's first public appearance in three years.

Since Lissa had left Paradise for the hospital in Phoenix with only the clothes on her back, the Henderson women had taken a hand in outfitting her for this momentous occasion. Sydney, with her filmmaker's eye for color and contrast, had decreed that the turquoise blouse and silver concho belt Evan's mom had offered looked perfect with her own black silk broomstick skirt. Molly had contributed the brand-new cowboy boots Sam had bought in hopes of making a rancher out of her one of these days. Lauren had come up with an exquisite pair of handcrafted silver-and-turquoise earrings.

Lissa had done her own hair and makeup. The heavily mascaraed, overpainted sex kitten with the mountains of teased curls was gone forever. She'd applied lip gloss and blush with a light hand, then swept her tawny mane up into a casually sophisticated twist. At the last minute, she'd brushed her bangs back from her face so they didn't hide her eyes. She wasn't hiding anything anymore.

Especially how she felt about Evan.

The love she couldn't hold back anymore

throbbed through her voice as she gave him a last chance to salvage his career.

"You don't have to go out there with me. I can handle it."

His arms slid around her waist. "You can handle anything, Ms. James."

Evan allowed himself one kiss, one long, intensely satisfying kiss, before he sprang the news of Marsh's arrival on her.

"Before we go downstairs, I think I should warn you that you'll be sharing the spotlight," he said with an apologetic smile. "Marsh just got here... with Doc."

She went rigid with shock. "What!"

"Customs picked him up a couple of hours ago, trying to cross the border with a fake ID. He, uh, had planned to meet with a stockbroker in El Paso to discuss his investments."

Doubt razored into Evan's gut for the second or two it took Lissa to recover from her shock. She'd fallen under the slick promoter's spell once. Did she harbor any residual feelings for the man?

The scorn that flashed in her eyes told him exactly what kind of feelings she harbored.

"Why in heaven's name did your brother bring Doc to the Bar-H?" she fumed. "He should have thrown him in jail and dropped the key down a sewer!"

"Well, I needed Dawes here to cut the deal I worked out with the Nashville D.A."

"Deal!" She pushed out of his arms, spitting fury. "You worked a deal for that worm?"

"In exchange for a minimum sentence of seven to ten years, your ex-manager has agreed to plead guilty to extortion and mail fraud…"

"How big of him!"

"…and admit you knew nothing about his scams," he finished calmly.

That took the wind from her sails. Her mouth opened, snapped shut, dropped open again. Grinning, Evan hustled her back into his arms.

"I figure it'll take a couple of months for Arlen's arm to heal well enough for him to escort you down the aisle. In the meantime, we'll use Doc's confession to reverse the judgment against you and decide where we're going to get married. If we do it here, we'll fly Reverend McNabb and his wife out so he can perform the ceremony."

Ruthlessly Evan took advantage of her stunned speechlessness to press ahead.

"Josephine and Charlie called this morning, by the way. Jo's volunteered to bake the wedding cake. She said to tell you she has this great recipe for an upside-down angel meringue, whatever that is."

Lissa's expression set laughter dancing in his heart.

"I know. It sounds pretty wild to me, too. But I can't think of anything more appropriate for an angel who's about to turn her life upside down all over again by marrying me."

"Who…?" The word spiraled into a squeak. Swallowing, Lissa started again. "Who said anything about marriage?"

"Well, Arlen for one. He let me know at the hospital he takes a dim view of any man messing around with his daughter. My mother, for another. She told me I'd be crazy not to get a rope around you as soon as I can. Then there's Reece and Marsh and Jake and…"

She stopped him by the simple expedient of slapping a palm over his mouth. Trapped behind the silken barrier, Evan planted a kiss on her warm, soft flesh.

"Never mind your brothers' take on the situation," she said breathlessly, removing her hand. "Just tell me what you think."

"There's no thinking involved, sweetheart. I fell in love with you so hard and so fast, my head still hasn't caught up with my heart."

"That's what I'm afraid of!"

Framing her worried face in his hands, Evan smiled down at her.

"All I know is that I want to spend the rest of my life with you…in our own special Paradise. Marry me, Lissa. Next week. Next month. Whenever you're ready and Josephine has that meringue whipped up."

* * *

The woman who strode out onto the flagstone patio some time later bore little resemblance to the country singing sensation once known as Missy Marie. Her hair was sliding free of its sleek twist. No trace of lipstick tinted lips that looked slightly swollen. Her lids weren't painted with the dramatic colors she once favored. Yet her brown eyes shone with a private joy that had photographers adjusting their lenses and grabbing for special filters to capture her glow.

She crossed the patio without even glancing at the handcuffed figure standing off to one side, guarded by two U.S. marshals. When she took her place behind the bank of microphones, five broad-shouldered Hendersons closed ranks behind her.

* * * * *

Look Who's Celebrating Our 20ᵗʰ Anniversary:

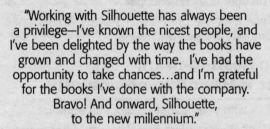

Celebrate 20 YEARS

"Working with Silhouette has always been a privilege—I've known the nicest people, and I've been delighted by the way the books have grown and changed with time. I've had the opportunity to take chances…and I'm grateful for the books I've done with the company. Bravo! And onward, Silhouette, to the new millennium."

—*New York Times* bestselling author
Heather Graham Pozzessere

"Twenty years of laughter and love... It's not hard to imagine Silhouette Books celebrating twenty years of quality publishing, but it is hard to imagine a publishing world without it. Congratulations..."

—International bestselling author
Emilie Richards

INTIMATE MOMENTS®
Silhouette®

SILHOUETTE'S 20ᵀᴴ ANNIVERSARY CONTEST
OFFICIAL RULES
NO PURCHASE NECESSARY TO ENTER

1. To enter, follow directions published in the offer to which you are responding. Contest begins 1/1/00 and ends on 8/24/00 (the "Promotion Period"). Method of entry may vary. Mailed entries must be postmarked by 8/24/00, and received by 8/31/00.

2. During the Promotion Period, the Contest may be presented via the Internet. Entry via the Internet may be restricted to residents of certain geographic areas that are disclosed on the Web site. To enter via the Internet, if you are a resident of a geographic area in which Internet entry is permissible, follow the directions displayed on-line, including typing your essay of 100 words or fewer telling us "Where In The World Your Love Will Come Alive." On-line entries must be received by 11:59 p.m. Eastern Standard time on 8/24/00. Limit one e-mail entry per person, household and e-mail address per day, per presentation. If you are a resident of a geographic area in which entry via the Internet is permissible, you may, in lieu of submitting an entry on-line, enter by mail, by hand-printing your name, address, telephone number and contest number/name on an 8"x 11" plain piece of paper and telling us in 100 words or fewer "Where In The World Your Love Will Come Alive," and mailing via first-class mail to: Silhouette 20ᵗʰ Anniversary Contest, (in the U.S.) P.O. Box 9069, Buffalo, NY 14269-9069; (In Canada) P.O. Box 637, Fort Erie, Ontario, Canada L2A 5X3. Limit one 8"x 11" mailed entry per person, household and e-mail address per day. On-line and/or 8"x 11" mailed entries received from persons residing in geographic areas in which Internet entry is not permissible will be disqualified. No liability is assumed for lost, late, incomplete, inaccurate, nondelivered or misdirected mail, or misdirected e-mail, for technical, hardware or software failures of any kind, lost or unavailable network connection, or failed, incomplete, garbled or delayed computer transmission or any human error which may occur in the receipt or processing of the entries in the contest.

3. Essays will be judged by a panel of members of the Silhouette editorial and marketing staff based on the following criteria:

   > Sincerity (believability, credibility)—50%
   > Originality (freshness, creativity)—30%
   > Aptness (appropriateness to contest ideas)—20%

   Purchase or acceptance of a product offer does not improve your chances of winning. In the event of a tie, duplicate prizes will be awarded.

4. All entries become the property of Harlequin Enterprises Ltd., and will not be returned. Winner will be determined no later than 10/31/00 and will be notified by mail. Grand Prize winner will be required to sign and return Affidavit of Eligibility within 15 days of receipt of notification. Noncompliance within the time period may result in disqualification and an alternative winner may be selected. All municipal, provincial, federal, state and local laws and regulations apply. Contest open only to residents of the U.S. and Canada who are 18 years of age or older, and is void wherever prohibited by law. Internet entry is restricted solely to residents of those geographical areas in which Internet entry is permissible. Employees of Torstar Corp., their affiliates, agents and members of their immediate families are not eligible. Taxes on the prizes are the sole responsibility of winners. Entry and acceptance of any prize offered constitutes permission to use winner's name, photograph or other likeness for the purposes of advertising, trade and promotion on behalf of Torstar Corp. without further compensation to the winner, unless prohibited by law. Torstar Corp and D.L. Blair, Inc., their parents, affiliates and subsidiaries, are not responsible for errors in printing or electronic presentation of contest or entries. In the event of printing or other errors which may result in unintended prize values or duplication of prizes, all affected contest materials or entries shall be null and void. If for any reason the Internet portion of the contest is not capable of running as planned, including infection by computer virus, bugs, tampering, unauthorized intervention, fraud, technical failures, or any other causes beyond the control of Torstar Corp. which corrupt or affect the administration, secrecy, fairness, integrity or proper conduct of the contest, Torstar Corp. reserves the right, at its sole discretion, to disqualify any individual who tampers with the entry process and to cancel, terminate, modify or suspend the contest or the Internet portion thereof. In the event of a dispute regarding an on-line entry, the entry will be deemed submitted by the authorized holder of the e-mail account submitted at the time of entry. Authorized account holder is defined as the natural person who is assigned to an e-mail address by an Internet access provider, on-line service provider or other organization that is responsible for arranging e-mail address for the domain associated with the submitted e-mail address.

5. Prizes: Grand Prize—a $10,000 vacation to anywhere in the world. Travelers (at least one must be 18 years of age or older) or parent or guardian if one traveler is a minor, must sign and return a Release of Liability prior to departure. Travel must be completed by December 31, 2001, and is subject to space and accommodations availability. Two hundred (200) Second Prizes—a two-book limited edition autographed collector set from one of the Silhouette Anniversary authors: Nora Roberts, Diana Palmer, Linda Howard or Annette Broadrick (value $10.00 each set). All prizes are valued in U.S. dollars.

6. For a list of winners (available after 10/31/00), send a self-addressed, stamped envelope to: Harlequin Silhouette 20ᵗʰ Anniversary Winners, P.O. Box 4200, Blair, NE 68009-4200.

Contest sponsored by Torstar Corp., P.O. Box 9042, Buffalo, NY 14269-9042.

PS20RULES

ENTER FOR A CHANCE TO WIN*

Silhouette's 20th Anniversary Contest

Tell Us Where in the World You Would Like *Your* Love To Come Alive... And We'll Send the Lucky Winner There!

Silhouette wants to take you wherever your happy ending can come true.

Here's how to enter: Tell us, in 100 words or less, where you want to go to make your love come alive!

In addition to the grand prize, there will be 200 runner-up prizes, collector's-edition book sets autographed by one of the Silhouette anniversary authors: **Nora Roberts, Diana Palmer, Linda Howard** or **Annette Broadrick**.

DON'T MISS YOUR CHANCE TO WIN! ENTER NOW! No Purchase Necessary

Silhouette®
Where love comes alive™

Visit Silhouette at www.eHarlequin.com to enter, starting this summer.

Name: _____

Address: _____

City: _____ State/Province: _____

Zip/Postal Code: _____

Mail to Harlequin Books: **In the U.S.**: P.O. Box 9069, Buffalo, NY 14269-9069; **In Canada**: P.O. Box 637, Fort Erie, Ontario, L4A 5X3

*No purchase necessary—for contest details send a self-addressed stamped envelope to: Silhouette's 20th Anniversary Contest, P.O. Box 9069, Buffalo, NY, 14269-9069 (include contest name on self-addressed envelope). Residents of Washington and Vermont may omit postage. Open to Cdn. (excluding Quebec) and U.S. residents who are 18 or over. Void where prohibited. Contest ends August 31, 2000.   PS20CON_R2